Split Seconds

Split Seconds

Kevin Robinson

Walker and Company
New York

First published in the United States of America in 1991
by Walker Publishing Company, Inc.
Published simultaneously in Canada by Thomas Allen & Son
Canada, Limited, Markham, Ontario

Library of Congress Cataloging-in-Publication Data
Robinson, Kevin.
Split seconds / Kevin Robinson.
p.   cm.
ISBN 0-8027-5785-5
I. Title.
PS3568.O2892S65   1991
813'.54—dc20   90-27185
CIP

Printed in the United States of America
2 4 6 8 10 9 7 5 3 1

92-00551

This book is dedicated to Harry Mark Petrakis. His stories and novels have always refreshed my spirit; his lessons have always increased my understanding; his encouragement has always fortified my resolve; and his loving friendship has always warmed my heart.

Acknowledgments

There are many people who helped this freelance writer become a "first novelist." I thank them all but will mention the contributions of just a few who stand out.

My wife, Shell, who was patient, and without whom . . .

My daughter, Melissa, who never doubted.

Paul and Shirley Kilpatrick, my first tutors.

Bob Albright, a wonderful actor, filled with great ideas and great encouragement.

Officer Jeff Roland, a *real* "good guy," who took the time to help.

Jim Forest, a *real* "computerhead," who knows his stuff and was willing to explain it . . . *way* down at my level.

Janet Hutchings, my editor, who bet on a longshot and then tirelessly helped us both narrow the odds.

The administration and staff at the Craig Spinal Rehabilitation Hospital in Englewood, Colorado, who help turn disability into ability . . . every day of their lives.

$\triangledown$

1

I HATE FUNERALS, SO I never go unless I have to. Suits and wheelchairs just don't go well together; and besides, I can't stand hanging out with sad people. But Jim Woods's funeral was different. First, it was germane to my first "real" newspaper story. It was business. Second, seeing the red-haired lady in the black lace dress was worth any discomfort my only necktie could impose. Katie Newman. Here was a woman you could die for. I wondered what she would say if she knew that I had her late fiancé's wallet hidden in the bottom of a twelve-pack of Preparation H, or that her wrinkled picture was pinned up in my office at home.

It was a hot afternoon in the west Orlando cemetery, and all but two people at the rear of the small crowd huddled in the shade of the green canvas grave-side tent. One of them looked at home in the sun and heat; the second looked almost shriveled, totally oppressed by Sol's relentless rays. I hung back, minimizing the lumbering return trip to my car. Aside from Katie, I noted Jim's parents and recognized Dave Bentley, but no one else rang any bells.

The preacher was a well-dressed, good-looking man in his forties who might have just stepped out of a Brooks Brothers'

window display. He had apparently known Jim well and
spoke at length about the computer wizard's Godly testi-
mony and faithful work with the youth of the small Orlando
church. When he addressed Gene and Edna Woods, it was
clear that they were close. Though his words carried succor
and comfort, grief among Woods's family flowed freely—with
one notable exception.

The young woman in black cried too, but carefully. She
held both Gene's and Edna's hand and had a white lace
handkerchief showing from under one sleeve. But there was
more than restraint in her hazel-green eyes and her tight-set
jaw. Miss Katie, if I am any observer of human nature, was
experiencing other manifestations of the grieving process. I
figured she was mad. But who could blame her?

In a church service, or any crowd setting, I learned early
on that living in a wheelchair means you have basically two
choices: you can be the first one out, or the last. There is
seldom any middle ground. As a result, I can spot a wrap-up
(or in this case, a benediction) from a mile away.

By the time the amen came drifting across the well-tended
Bahia grass, I was pulling my ultralight folding chair into
the backseat of my salt-air ravaged '86 Z28. The battered
Camaro wasn't pretty anymore, but she could still fly. The
trip back to the coast on the Bee Line Expressway would be
cathartic. After hauling in my useless legs and fastening the
safety belt, I cranked up the 350-cubic-inch, fuel-injected
engine and checked the cemetery road for oncoming grievers.
The lady in black was right there at my elbow, leaning in to
address me face-to-face. I swallowed my gum.

"You're Mr. Nick Foster, aren't you?"

"Stick," I said, trying vainly not to look startled. "People
just call me Stick."

"I'm Katie Newman, Jim Woods's fiancée. Edna, Jim's
Mom, showed me your column in the paper. She's pretty
upset, of course, and I'd like to talk to you about it. May I?"

She motioned to the passenger seat and started around the car.

"Sure," I said to the empty window. It didn't look as if I had any choice. Who am I kidding? I didn't want a choice. I tossed a crumpled Burger Man bag into the back and brushed a couple of loose french fries off the other seat and onto the floor.

"I told Gene to go on," Katie said, getting in. "Can you drop me off on your way through town?"

I saw it in the dictionary—as Katie's long legs flowed gracefully into the front seat beside me—nestled somewhere between *formic acid* and *form letter*. *Formidable: tending to inspire awe or wonder.*

"Of course," I said. There didn't seem to be any good reason to tell her that I hadn't planned on going through town at all, so I pulled out on Highway 50 and drove east—just slightly under the posted speed.

"Gene says it was probably an accident," Katie said, shifting to face me, resting her knees against the cellular car phone, which was Velcro-mounted on the console. "He hates conflict, just wants to be done with it all. Jimmy's brothers swim like fish—both of them are weekend surfers—but Jim didn't go in much for the water. Edna and I think that you are right, Mr. Foster. In fact, I know you're right."

Now she was really crying, at least fighting off real tears. I engaged the cruise control and fished around on the dashboard for a napkin without too much dust or catsup on it. "Here," I said. "And call me Stick."

Isn't there something in the Bible about consoling widows? Katie Newman wasn't technically a widow, but I wanted the job anyway. Trouble was, I couldn't think of anything consoling to say. So I just left her alone.

"How does this work?" she asked, seconds later when the battle for composure was apparently won.

"What?"

"The car. You're using just your hands."

"That's why they're called hand controls," I said, surprised by the sudden change in subject. "Down for gas. Toward the dash for brakes."

"I'm sorry," she said, dabbing at her eyes with the napkin. "I've never ridden with anyone who was . . ."

"In a chair?" I inserted into the familiar pause.

"Yes, in a chair."

"I know this whole thing stinks, Miss Newman," I said, opting to help her out of the hole she was digging, "but if you know something about Jim's death, you probably need to talk to the police."

"How far did you get?" she asked. Her glistening green eyes narrowed, total control returning immediately.

"Frankly, not very far."

"Well, I've been down that same short road. Look, Mr. Foster, I don't know anybody else down here, but Edna says you know everybody. I need your help."

"Call me Stick."

"Turn here."

Yes, ma'am.

It was rush hour by the time I left the tree-lined Winter Park neighborhood where Gene and Edna Woods lived. The rusty blue Z28 hates rush hour but did her best to hasten my trip out of town. I took Highway 50 out to 520 and followed that south, getting on Interstate 95 at Cocoa. The Route 192 exit runs right into Melbourne.

Katie Newman had good enough reason to believe that Jim met with foul play. The week before he died, he'd called to say that he had discovered "something odd" at work—somebody, maybe, tampering with his software. She told me that Jim sounded nervous, even though he assured her it would all be straightened out before he flew up for their planned weekend in Kansas City—a trip scheduled, by ne-

cessity, for right after the next space shuttle carried its payload into earth orbit. The shuttle program, long grounded
after the *Challenger* tragedy, was back in business in a big
way. Flights came and went routinely; delays—to NASA's
great delight—were few and far between. Unfortunately,
Katie's next phone call came from Edna Woods.

Still, as I had tried to point out, Katie's revelation, without
some hard evidence to support it, wasn't much good to the
police, or to me. But oh yes, I would do my best. I left her
my numbers—at the paper, at home, and in the car—and
promised to get back to her. A promise I would have no trouble keeping.

I didn't tell her about the wallet.

$\triangledown$

2

ALTHOUGH I HAVEN'T STOOD upright since 1986, I *was* six-foot-four. Sometimes I'm tempted to answer strangers' questions by telling them I was wounded in Nam, or that I turned over in a jeep while competing in the Pikes Peak Hill Climb Race. But I can never bring myself to tell such a bold-faced lie, so I reluctantly admit that I fell off the garage roof while helping my Dad replace the shingles.

In high school some of the shorter kids called me Nick the Stick. I hated it back then, but when I decided to try my hand at journalism, Stick started to sound pretty good. I've handled the Shore Line feature for the *Melbourne Sun Coaster* for just over two years now, and while my column is picked up regularly by several mid-Florida newspapers, I thought the crabbing piece might have a good shot at national syndication. "Working" at my stories is my trademark and has helped me collect both readers and friends all over central Florida.

" 'Stick' is good," my editor, Randy White, once said. "People just seem to stick to you, Foster. I don't begin to know how you get them to adopt you, let alone go along with your hair-brained ideas. But it makes for good copy."

"It's not my fault," I told him, "if it's harder to say no to someone in a wheelchair."

Finding Jim Woods's body would not be the brightest memory of my journalistic career. His hand—or what was left of it—broke the surface first. The flesh was badly torn and frayed, but the striped Oxford shirtsleeve looked almost new. The light blue material was caught, in several places, on the bent-wire edges of the crab trap.

Phil nearly went overboard as he yelled for me to stop. I slipped the old outboard into reverse and backed up slowly while Phil brought the unusual catch alongside. The trap was badly stretched, from the upper corner where the yellow nylon rope that connected it to its buoy was tied, to the opposite edge where most of the dead man's sleeve was caught. Despite being damaged, the trap was full of blue crabs.

Crabbing was Phillip Stilles's second job. He was, by trade, a mechanic. If it had moving parts, he could fix it. Otherwise, he had little use for it. The sixty-five horsepower Merc that pushed his twenty-foot wooden scow should have died with dignity years ago, but Phil got to it first. Each morning he coaxed it to life with the skill of a heart surgeon and the delicacy of a blacksmith.

Stilles never even hesitated when I asked him to let me tag along for a week or so. I liked him right away, and our friendship grew quickly, but we made a strange team. In the beginning, everyone at the docks stopped what they were doing to watch us go to work—a short hulk of a man carrying boxes of bait that were usually carried by two men, and a paralyzed reporter with brown hair, hazel eyes, and a tidy beard, who left his wheelchair under a tree by the marina store and scooted down the dock on his backside. But the novelty wore off after a few days. Soon we were just another crew, scrambling to make a living by trapping and selling the sumptuous blue crabs that inhabit the warm and salty depths of Florida's Intercoastal Waterway.

I hadn't been at the crab game for quite a week before I had the system down. The principle is simple. Keep the boat moving steadily but as quickly as possible, allowing only enough time for your partner to grab the buoy line, pull the trap on board, empty its contents, refill the bait well, and drop it back in the water—just in time to catch the next trap in the line. The actual practice is somewhat more difficult, and stopping or circling back is considered most unprofessional.

That morning, after Phil dropped the last southern trap back in the water, I headed north up the channel as fast as the old tub would go. Soon after we passed under the Melbourne bridge, we ran by the first buoys of Phillip's second line. The Styrofoam floats were orange and royal blue, with his permit number burned into each.

I pulled around the most northern trap and while Phil hauled it up, I looked for Propjob. The old dolphin with the scarred-up head met us there every day. When Phil fed him a pogy or two, rubbed his shiny gray snout, and wished him a good day, the graceful creature would sing briefly, show off with a jump or two, and disappear. On several occasions, Phil told me, Propjob brought him empty beer cans or old pieces of anchor rope. A "thank you" perhaps. I was waiting for him to surface when the boat lugged down suddenly and Phil shouted at me from the stern. It wasn't Propjob, but it was going to be a long day.

Switching on the ship-to-shore, I called the water patrol and the paper. Sometimes they really do "stop the presses." Then we dropped anchor to wait. Phil tied off the rope—I insisted that he not bring his new friend on board—and the pale ragged hand waved grotesquely, just above the light chop of the warm green water. The nearest water patrol officers were six miles north when I called, but their craft was designed for a different kind of work than Phil's, and they pulled up alongside us only moments later. After lashing the jet-boat to our starboard side, one of them asked Phillip's permission to come aboard. It struck me as funny, somehow, under the circumstances, but I didn't laugh.

While Phil answered questions, I took note of their perfectly pressed uniforms and got a better look at the shiny clean speedboat. I was just starting to get a picture of these two loading our dead mate into their spiffy cruiser—it would prove to be a most grizzly entertainment—when a larger craft, bearing the seal of the Brevard County coroner's office, pulled up to portside. The crew was dressed in white lab coats, and the boat was fitted with several pieces of stainless-steel equipment obviously designed for just such a task. There was another story, for another day.

When they all left, Phil straightened out the damaged trap as best he could and emptied its still-snapping contents into the burlap-lined box at his feet. The north line—with the exception of that ill-fated trap—was doing poorly. Phil lifted the last half-dozen traps and we carried them down to the closest end of his southern string. It was after noon when we finally turned into the mouth of the inlet where the marina lay sheltered from the main body of the Intercoastal Waterway.

"Funny thing about that guy," Phil said as we glided into the docks.

"Yeah, it's too bad. I wonder how it happened."

"Huh? Oh, no, I didn't mean that," he said. "Did you notice how many crabs were in that trap? I've never done that well on pogies!"

"You're sick," I said as he loaded the crabs into his truck and soaked down the burlap box covers for the trip to the wholesale fish house nearby.

James Woods, I found out later that afternoon, had been a twenty-seven-year-old computer specialist with Com-Tech, attached to NASA at the Kennedy Space Center. According to a spokesperson there, he worked with the emergency fail-safe software responsible for destroying any launch vehicle that goes haywire and threatens to turn back toward land. It was Jim's program that, at the last possible second, transmitted the destruct command when the ill-fated *Challenger*'s auxiliary boosters arced back toward the cape after the shuttle itself exploded unexpectedly.

Suddenly, my friendly crab story was on hiatus, and I was getting my first shot at some serious journalism. The next morning, instead of piloting Phillip's scow up the Intercoastal Waterway, I steered my rusty blue Z28 Camaro through the back guard gate at the cape.

"So you're Nick Foster," said the young PR man, with rolled-up sleeves, red suspenders, and a narrow teal-colored necktie. "I don't take the Melbourne paper, but I've heard about you. My name is Dave. I didn't know you were—"

"In a chair?" I said.

"In a chair," he repeated, smiling with unnecessary discomfort and embarrassment.

"And call me Stick, okay?"

Com-Tech's public relations man, Dave Bentley, gave me a brief tour of computer operations, ending up at Jim Woods's desk.

"This was Jim's main office," Dave said. "But he sometimes worked down at the tracking station too.

"Jim was a character," he said, shaking his head sadly at the exasperated Garfield that clung, splayed out in panicked desperation on suction-cupped paws, to the cubicle's glass-topped wall.

A computer-generated pennant behind the desk spoke more succinctly about the late occupant's wit. COM-TECH, it said in proud, bold letters, SOLVING TOMORROW'S PROBLEMS USING YESTERDAY'S TECHNOLOGY.

"It's a lousy break," Dave went on. "Jim was one of our brightest computerheads. Do you know what he did for a living before he started here?"

I shook my head.

"He worked the night shift at a Majik Markit convenience store in Orlando. Can you imagine, minimum wage to forty grand. Overnight."

I rolled around the cluttered office and was suddenly struck by a framed photograph so compelling, I just parked my wheelchair behind the desk and stared.

"That's Katie," Dave said. "They were engaged to be married this Christmas."

The red-haired woman with French braids looked out at me with bright green eyes. Her smile made the sun shine, and she had the sexiest freckles I'd ever seen.

"She lives in Kansas City," Dave said quietly. "She'll probably be down for the funeral."

"Tell me about his work," I said, unable to look away from the photograph.

Dave brightened. "The technology was here. Basically, it's a matter of high-tech communication. That is, computers here talking to on-board computers making the trip. Every bird's trajectory is bounded by a set of imaginary lines. If the flight remains within the lines, fine. But if it strays, even a little, something has to be done—fast.

"Woods's specialty was parallel processing—programming the computer in a way that enables it to handle two or more operations simultaneously. We were working on that already, but Jim moved our technique ahead by light years. NASA has explosive charges on every crate that lifts off here, you know, in case it goes outside the lines. Blowing stuff up is no problem, but ground command and the range safety officers—the one's who actually push the button—want as much time as possible to try for a fix first. So, being able to hold off until the last possible second—actually, millisecond—has been the challenge.

"A millisecond," Dave continued, as if he were addressing a group of schoolchildren on a field trip, "is one-thousandth of a second, and with some semipirated Morton Manufacturing and Aerospace software, Com-Tech had the whole procedure down to a couple of milliseconds. Jim Woods walked in here, literally off the street, and had us thinking in nanoseconds. That's *billionths* of a second. It's actually a better measurement of how fast the computers themselves can work."

"Where did he learn to do that?" I asked, finally impressed enough to look away from the redhead.

"Oh, he went to school, but guys like Jim don't learn, per se," Dave said with a grin. "High-tech magic just seems to come to them. I know that sounds funny, but genuine computerheads aren't like regular people. Their minds float around in the upper atmosphere where the real world never goes.

"When Jim was eight, or so he told me, he sent his first electronic chess computer back to the manufacturer to be upgraded—six times! The joke around here was that Jimmy was 'one' with the mainframe. Even Katie used to say that she'd only be his mistress. His computer was his first love."

"So who might kill him for his knowledge?"

Dave Bentley got real still and looked at me as if I'd just told an obscene joke to his grandmother.

"The police said it was probably just a boating accident," he said at last.

"Did he own a boat?"

"I don't think so."

"Talk boating, fishing, and the like?"

"Well, no—"

"I didn't think so, " I said. "Doesn't strike me as the type. Besides, he wasn't dressed for it."

$\triangledown$

3

THAT NIGHT, WHEN MY favorite crabman, Phillip Stilles, called and informed me that I wanted to go shrimping with him, I almost told him what to do with his outboard. I had just pulled off my shoes and settled into my easy chair for the evening. Butkis, my brown Tonkinese cat, was already snoozing on my wheelchair seat cushion, and Senator Benjamin Holcum was holding yet another press conference on TV.

I had never paid much attention to his anti-space-program rhetoric before, but in light of my new story, I thought it wise to listen more carefully. "Since 1968," he was saying dramatically, "we have spent four hundred and fifty billion dollars on war, ninty-five billion dollars on space, and less than six billion dollars on urban development, public assistance, and low-income housing."

"I read your column tonight," Phil said, interrupting the overweight southern orator, "but you seem to be all alone in your suggestion of foul play."

"So what do they know?"

"Does our friend Woods have a middle name that starts with 'E'?"

"Edward. Why?"

"Let's go shrimping. I'll meet you at the marina in half an hour."

I idled the old Merc while Phil brought the truck battery and the spotlights on board.

"Went last night," he said as he cast off the lines. "Not many shrimp, but I thought you might be interested in some of the other night fishing on the river."

A warm night on the Intercoastal is almost surreal. The dark salty water—smelling of both life and death—is dotted with light from a hundred swinging lanterns and spotlights. Along the shorelines, the net fishermen work the shallows for pogies and mullet, their lanterns hissing softly over the gunwales. Ghostlike shrimp trawlers haunt the main channel, their great net-bearing arms—strung with bare, clear glass light bulbs—dip to either side as they pass slowly by.

Free-lancers like Phil, looking for a bargain-priced pot full of ready-to-be-boiled shrimp, anchor just out of the channel. Automobile headlights, wired to alligator clips and clamped to old car or truck batteries, hang out over the flowing water while the would-be shrimpers stand or sit, holding long-handled aluminum dipping nets. The shrimp—when they are "running"—are carried along at the surface, looking like little pink Kilroys, their beady periscope eyes alert for danger.

Sounds and voices carry across the saltwater in a way that makes distances deceptive. After Phil signaled me to cut the engine and drop anchor, he set out the lights and stood up in the stern with his shrimp net in hand. We were about a hundred yards downwind of his northern string of buoys, and I knew that whatever we were doing had little to do with shrimp. Phil would clue me when and if he felt like it.

We both dipped our nets several times before I noticed a sound that didn't fit properly into the late night cacophony. Amid the chorus of dipping nets, whispered conversations, and chaffing anchor lines, came a series of splashes from a boat near the head of Phil's trap line. When the hollow-wet sound of clearing air lines drifted toward us, I reached into the box under the pilot's chair and unwrapped Phillip's binoculars.

"Careful," he whispered.

I set the thermos up on the bait well behind me and tried to be subtle about peeking around it with the glasses. The boat anchored upstream was using kerosene lanterns, and the man in the bow wasn't dipping his net. I lowered the binoculars and splashed with my own net when his watchful gaze turned our way.

"Missed!" Phil chided, his back purposely to the suspicious craft. He scooped up a lone shrimp and tapped his net upside down into the cooler on the deck between us. "How about those Miami Dolphins? Think they'll make good this year?"

"Hard to say," I answered, raising the glasses in time to see a diver's face mask slip below the surface and to hear the rush of air bubbles along the other boat's portside. The eerie blue-green glow that spread softly across the dark water announced that a spotlight had been turned on below. Unless I was mistaken, the tall man in the bow was wearing a sports coat over a flowery shirt; he looked out of place, nervously scanning the night around him. When the breeze swung his boat a few degrees about, I saw that it was long and low to the water—an inboard, maybe a jet.

"Kind of slow tonight," I said, dipping at nothing.

"You want to quit already?" Phil laughed. "I don't know why I invite you along. If the shrimp don't jump right in the boat, you want to go home and watch television."

"It beats this. I could catch as many shrimp in the bathtub."

"How many times do I have to tell you," Phil said, unhooking the lights, "those are body crabs."

A few moments later, we swung into the shadowy marina.

"All right, what was that all about? And who was that diving on your traps?"

"You're a real-life investigative reporter now," Phil chuckled. "I figured you'd tell me."

"I take it they were here last night."

"Yup," Phil said as he leaned out to catch the dock.

"And they apparently didn't finish up."

"Good for you! You're showing definite promise."

"Oh, lay off," I snapped, throwing the dead weight of my lower body out onto the dock. Phil was enjoying the suspense routine just a little bit too much for my taste. "Wouldn't it be easier to dive during the day?"

"Not if you don't want to draw attention to yourself."

"There is that," I agreed. "So how did you know they'd come back tonight?"

"Two reasons. First, I walked out on the bridge before I called you," he said, grinning and pointing at the looming structure. "Just to be sure. But second, since they didn't have what they were looking for, I wasn't surprised to find them at it again."

"How do you know what they were looking for, let alone whether or not they found it?"

"That's easy," Phil said with undisguised pleasure. "Because I have it!"

The blue nylon wallet with black trim and Velcro closures was still damp. The initials embossed on the flap read J.E.W.

"I didn't think it was an ethnic reference," Phil said sarcastically.

"How in the world did you get it?"

"Strangest thing. It was personally delivered to me this morning while I was making my run without you." Phil's grin grew even bigger. "By my good friend, Propjob T. Porpoise." The *T* stands for "the."

* * *

Back at the house, I nuked some coffee water in the micro-wave while Phil used paper towels and a blow dryer on the wallet's sodden contents. Butkis looked on with disgust. He is suspicious of the smell of seawater, and it was well past his bedtime.

"So this guy was a high-ranking nerd," Phil said. "As bad as that is, it's a shame to get killed for it."

"At least you and I don't need to worry about getting knocked off for being too smart," I quipped.

"Speak for yourself."

With one exception, everything in Jim Woods's wallet was pretty straightforward: driver's license; Social Security card; MasterCard, VISA, and Discover charge plates; an Orange County library card; thirty-two dollars in cash; and a picture of the redhead, Katie, which I noticed Phil was taking great pains to salvage.

The odd item out was a shiny gold disc measuring just more than two inches across. It didn't take a genius to figure out what the *Miami Vice* types were diving for.

"Looks like a gold record award for midgets," Phil said, laughing.

"Little people," I corrected him.

"Little people then. What do you think it is?"

"It's a laser disc, I'm sure, like the compact laser discs they sell for high-dollar stereos, only smaller. Much smaller."

"You mean for midg—little people?"

"Very little people," I said, "or very high-tech computers."

$\triangledown$

4

"Y OU WEREN'T AT PRACTICE last night. You promised."

"I'm sorry, Sam. I had to go shrimping."

"Well, that's different then. Come on, Stick, you said your next story would be about the Wheels."

"Sam, I'm hurt. I thought you wanted me for my hook shot."

"I'm not discussing what I want you for. We've been through that. But the team really needs some PR, and you can give it to them."

The Orlando Orange Wheels are one of the best teams in the southeast conference of the National Wheelchair Basketball Association. And Samantha Wagner is the hottest player–business manager anywhere. She almost dresses for the tropics, and her golden sun-bleached hair falls across her deeply tanned shoulders in a most disconcerting way. Not surprisingly, some guys never notice her wheelchair at all.

The fact that Sam lives life to the fullest deceives some of her admirers into thinking she's more of a free spirit than she is. She has her M.B.A. from the University of Central Florida and is well on her way to a law degree at Stetson. Her looks and her life-style, however, might account for a long list of young men with broken hearts. If rumors were to be believed—and I saw no reason why they shouldn't be—a night in Samantha's arms could make a fellow forget "able-bodied" women altogether. Her insistent invitations were not lost on me, but I just wasn't ready to become another in her long line of conquests.

"All right, Sam, I'll tell you what I'll do. You get me an appointment with your brother—over at the Morton plant—and I'll be at practice next week."

"And Saturday's game? It's home."

"And Saturday's game."

"Promise?"

"Promise."

"And then dinner?"

"Maybe."

"Okay, it's a deal."

I felt her smile burning through the phone line before I hung up. I took a cold shower.

The next morning, Sam's brother met me in the security office at the Morton defense-manufacturing complex in southwest Orlando.

"Hi, Stick. Sam's told me a lot about you. She says you play hard to get—either that, or you're gay!"

Jerry Wagner is what Dave Bentley would call a computer-head and talking to him is intimidating enough without trying to hide a blush. He laughed at my instantaneous denial and pushed the red tortoiseshell glasses back up his slender nose.

"Don't worry about it," he quipped. "Little sister never stays serious about the ones who come too easy." He shrugged his shoulders. "And that seems to be just about everybody but you. Ever since her injury, Sam seems to, I don't know, overcompensate? Especially after her jerk-of-a-husband walked. Is that common with disabled folks?"

"Sometimes, I guess." I never even knew she'd been married.

"She didn't tell you," Jerry said, looking at me more closely. "Two years of wedded bliss—their first two at UCF. But his career track didn't allow for being a nurse. He just went on like Sam never existed. Come on back to my office."

Unlike Jim Woods's cubicle at Com-Tech, Jerry's office was an office. It even had a door and a window.

"That's one of the test ranges," he said, pointing to a bowl-shaped depression in the earth. "It's almost a mile away, but when they're blowing up tanks or something out there, the windows shake."

In the distance, I saw several triangular signs mounted in various treetops. If anything was written on them, it was too small to see.

"Laser targeting research from the seventies," Jerry said, noticing my gaze. "Nobody ever bothered to take them down."

"How big a deal was it getting me in here?" I asked, fingering the ID badge clipped to my shirt pocket.

"Not bad," he grinned, "but I wouldn't get caught hanging out with any Middle Eastern types for a while. And, no kidding, don't write any exposés on Morton. We could both find ourselves in hot water. Why did you want to see me here anyway?"

I looked at the walls around us. "Can we talk, Jerry? I mean privately?"

"Who knows?" he shrugged. "I suppose Morton Manufacturing and Aerospace is second only to the Pentagon for paranoia. If it has to be here, you'll have to take your chances. I really don't know."

"Can I find out what's on this someplace else?" I set the tiny laser disc on his desk and watched Jerry's eyes get big.

"Where did you get that?" Now he was looking at the walls. "Is it one of ours? Somebody's in real deep."

"I don't even know what it is," I said, "but I figure it has something to do with computers . . . probably at the cape. It came out of the Intercoastal."

"The dead guy from Com-Tech?"

I nodded my head and Jerry looked relieved.

"Can you tell me what's on it?" I asked.

"Maybe. Maybe not."

Jerry explained that what I had was the absolute latest in a series of miniaturized laser data storage discs. A very recent arrival at Morton. Only a handful of industries had access to the hardware, he told me, but Com-Tech would likely have been one of them. His office machine wasn't set up for it, but one of his cronies apparently worked with the laser technology every day.

"Lots smaller, lots more data," said the short, wizened lady Jerry introduced as Trish Taylor. "Over six hundred million bits of information will fit on one of these."

"That's what the industry's always pushing for," Jerry added. "Today, stuff that used to take up whole buildings will fit in the glove box of your car."

"Or in your pocket," I said.

"Or in your pocket," Trish repeated, taking the glittering disc to her desktop terminal. "There have been regular-size laser ROM discs around for several years. You know, Read Only Memory. But this little baby," she said, pointing to a small gray box tethered to her computer's central processor unit, "is one of the first read-write units. With this gadget, I can put data on and take data off just as if it were an old floppy disk—well, more like dozens of floppy disks."

The gray laser gizmo on Trish's desk was slightly different from the one I had seen hooked to Jim Woods's computer. In fact, I had dismissed the other as a tape backup or some such. Now, despite the disparity in size and color, there was little doubt in my mind that Jim and Trish were similarly outfitted with the high-tech laser gadgetry.

"The format at Com-Tech is bound to be different," Trish went on, "and every programmer has a unique style, so don't expect much right off."

"Now you know why Trish's been here for fifteen years," Jerry laughed. "She knows how to cover her tail."

Trish Taylor's bony fingers sped gracefully across the keyboard.

"Only two files on here," she said. "Or rather, the same file twice. Let's see what it looks like." Her fingers danced again.

"There it is," she said, when a stream of amber gibberish rolled down her screen. "When all else is gone, data lives."

"How do you know the two programs are the same? And what does all that chicken scratch mean?" I asked.

"That," Trish smiled, "I cannot, or rather will not, tell you. I have too much work of my own to do. Get Jerry to do it if you can . . . on his own time. As to your other question, since the two programs take up the identical number of storage bytes, odds are that one is just a backup of the other. I'd print you up a hard copy, but we're talking several phone books' worth of programming code.

"I'll keep a copy here on my hard drives—Jerry can access it from there—but I'd hang on to this if I were you," Trish said, handing me the disc. "It's worth a small fortune no matter what's on it."

"Don't I know it," I said soberly. "One person has already paid with his life." The next afternoon was Jim Woods's funeral.

$\triangledown$

5

I WAS STILL HAVING trouble putting the memory of Katie
Newman's black dress out of my mind. Her musky perfume
lingered—drowning, for a time, the smell of lost onion rings
and a half-eaten Big Burger. I arrived home from Woods's
funeral to a driveway full of police cars. There was an ambulance on the front lawn, and Phil's pickup truck was
parked across the street. My front door stood open, so Butkis,
at least, was probably long gone.

Officer Alfonzo "the Fonze" Sanchez met me as I came up
the ramp to my front porch. He is a compact ex-marine who
has served on the Melbourne police force for twelve years. I
rode the graveyard shift for a week with him in the spring,
and it turned out to be one of my better stories. Now he was
telling me that Phillip Stilles had been shot.

"He's going to be okay," he assured me. "He just walked
into your place at the wrong time. I guess the guys trashing
it were armed for a gimp, not a bull elephant!"

Inside, Phil was contending with the emergency medical
technicians. I had spent a week riding one of the local meat
wagons too, but didn't recognize the crew in my living room.

"What happened here?" was all I could think to ask. My
house was in shambles. Phil sat grinning, sloughing off the

stretcher and the ride to the emergency room that was being recommended by the ambulance crew and ignoring a second police officer still trying to ask him questions. He had also bled on my favorite chair, but the bleeding seemed to be under control.

"It's just a scratch," he said, indicating the bandage on his ribs. "The bullet's over there." He pointed to the plainclothesman using a penknife on my homemade bookshelves. "You should see the big guy's nose. I rearranged it permanently!"

"What big guy? Phil, what's going on?"

"The other one," he said with delight, "I think I broke the little crater-faced mullet's arm. Boy, that was fun!"

Phil had boxed some in the navy, and the thought of catching one of his gnarled fists made me shudder. He was—pound for pound—the strongest man I'd ever known.

"Hey, earth calling Rambo! What happened to my house? Who's the 'crater-faced mullet,' and where is he now?"

"Gone." Phillip smiled and waved his hand in celestial satisfaction. "Off somewhere nursing a broken arm!"

I tried the Fonze. "What gives here anyway? Why is my house suddenly a combat zone?"

"Mr. Stilles here says he just walked in on them—two men—and they were apparently burglarizing your house."

"Apparently?"

"Since they were interrupted," Officer Sanchez went on with a shrug, "there's probably nothing missing, but you'd better take a look around anyway. Mr. Stilles says they weren't carrying anything on their way out the door. Seems they left in a hurry. Mr. a.k.a. 'Mullet' even left that behind." The Fonze pointed to a snub-nosed .38 special in a clear plastic bag on my end table.

"You should have seen his eyes," Phil cackled, "when I reached out and took it away from him . . . nearly arm and all!"

I worked my way through the rubble, shoving aside lamps and books to make a path for my wheelchair. The intruders had left no bric-a-brac unturned. The only items of any real value in my house are my word processor, my stereo, and my spare wheelchair. These were untouched, but my stereo cassettes and my floppy disks were strewn everywhere. With the Fonze following me around, looking over my shoulder, it seemed best to check the Preparation H later.

"More like they were looking for something," he said nonchalantly. "Wouldn't you say?"

"Maybe something I wrote," I said, bending down across my lap to scoop up a half-dozen floppies. "I've ticked a few people off before. No, I've got it! They were fans, just looking for a piece of famous writer memorabilia!"

"Come on, Stick. There must be more to it than that. Even bona fide residential house thieves don't carry guns. It's an automatic five years in this state."

"I've always liked that law."

"Stick . . ."

"Okay, Fonze, look. Your fraternal brothers at homicide aren't interested in my suggestions that the computer wiz from Com-Tech was murdered. Maybe someone else is."

"Great."

After a phone call to the station, a brief wait, and a return call, the Fonze informed us that Jim Woods's Orlando bungalow had been ransacked earlier in the day.

"Looks like you've got yourself a real live investigation now." Sanchez smiled.

Thanks for nothing.

When the circus moved on, and after I had chucked my sports coat and checked the house again, I joined Phil in the living room—the middle of the disaster area that had once been my moderately well ordered home.

"You okay?" I asked.

"Sure."

"Were they the same two we saw out on the river?"

"Five'll get you ten."

"What gave them the idea that I had it? Do you think they made us the other night?"

"Maybe," Phil said, "but this isn't bad either." He picked up the paper and read aloud. "Despite the present contention of law enforcement officials, there may be evidence to suggest that James Woods met with foul play. Information passed to this reporter suggests that Mr. Woods may have have been in possession of work-related materials important enough to have gotten him killed."

"It didn't seem all that threatening when I wrote it."

"Ah, Stick, you've a flair for the dramatic. You might just make it as a real reporter yet. But are you tough enough to protect your source? Something like this could come down hard on poor old Propjob."

"I have a second source now," I said, and I told him about my afternoon with Katie Newman.

"It looks like we'd all better watch our backsides for a while," he said.

"Remind me to work on that."

"Looks like you already do," Phil said, chuckling. "I love it . . . Preparation H!"

"Look, if you were stuck on your butt all day, you'd need it too."

A dark brown face appeared on the wrong side of the screen door, followed by a short, bratty whine. When I opened the door, Butkis surveyed the scene with distaste, jumped lightly onto my lap, and went promptly to sleep. He'd had quite enough trauma for one day. Thank you very much.

Phil excused himself, still chuckling, and before he had crossed the front lawn on the way to his truck, he was doing a terrible Johnny Cash impersonation. "I fell into a burning ring of fire. I sat down, down, down, and the flames got higher . . ."

Smart aleck.

* * *

After widening the path through the debris in my living room and along the bookshelves in the hall, I returned to my office and began putting things back in order. I would file two stories with Randy for the Friday edition. One on the break-in, and one for Shore Line on the James Woods case. "Big guy" and "Mullet" would play prominently in both. The police would, I hoped, take up the chase in earnest before anybody else got hurt.

None of my hardware or software seemed any the worse for wear, and the twenty-meg hard drive kicked into gear nicely when I cranked up my old NCR personal computer. On the wall in front of me hangs an array of familiar items: a framed marquee ad that announces TONIGHT ONLY, FEATURING JAKE AND ELWOOD BLUES AND THE BLUES BROTHERS BAND. BACK AFTER 3 YEARS, FABULOUS RHYTHM AND BLUES REVUE; a small wooden plaque that says SOME-TIMES I SITS AND THINKS . . . AND SOMETIMES I JUST SITS. and a stretched fabric picture of a sunset at the beach.

On the wall to the left of my desk is my not-so-tidy bul-letin board. Some of the memos and reminders held there by pushpins are two years old. I keep intending to bring it up to date, but there always seems to be just enough room to tack up one more note . . . or picture.

I searched the floor along the wall and under my desk. Katie Newman's picture was gone.

$\triangledown$

6

"I'M SO GLAD you warned us, Mr. Foster." Gene Woods was calling me back at 1 A.M.

"Stick. Call me Stick. Did you phone the police?"

"Edna dialed 911 while I talked to them through the door. They didn't fool me," said Gene Woods, on the other end of the line, "flashing phony ID badges and saying they were police detectives. I tried to keep them talking, but when the sirens came down the street, they took off in a hurry. I gave their descriptions to the officers—just like you said—a big one with a nose like a bad mushroom and a little pock-marked fellow with his arm in a sling.

"Mr. Foster, did those men kill my boy?"

"I don't know, Mr. Woods," I told him honestly enough. "Please, call me Stick. How's Katie?"

"She's a little shaken, of course, but Katie's a tough cookie. The police left a patrol car parked on the street outside, so we're not too worried about anything more tonight. I was wondering though," he said, pausing awkwardly, "I mean, I know I didn't think much of your suggestions early on, but right is right. And I surely appreciate your calling earlier tonight, but anyway, if you could see yourself clear to do me another favor, I'd be mighty obliged."

28

"What is it, Mr. Woods?"

"Well, Edna and Katie are driving down to Jupiter tomorrow, to get Jimmy's things at the motel, and I'd feel better if you would sort of meet them there—I could take off work, but—"

"Excuse me, Mr. Woods," I'd been perilously close to drifting back to sleep, but he had my attention now. "What motel? Why would your son have things at a motel in Jupiter . . . a hundred miles south of the cape?"

"Ah, well, there's a tracking station down there—at the Jonathan Dickenson State Park. Sometimes things get all in a rush, you know, lift-off schedules and the like. Jimmy would often spend thirteen or fourteen hours a day on the job, and then have to commute the three-plus hours back here. I guess Com-Tech didn't want him to end up in a ditch along the turnpike, so they kept a room for him at the Riverside Inn."

"Did you tell the police? Anyone?"

"No, I don't think so. It isn't something that came up . . . until Katie got to asking about the stuffed bear she'd bought for Jimmy's birthday. He called it Baby Bear. Why, he kept that—"

"Mr. Woods?" I interrupted.

"Uh, yes?"

"I'll be glad to meet them. What time?"

"Oh, well, how's ten, then?"

"Ten is fine. Good night, Mr. Woods."

"Oh, yes, well thank you very much. Good night, Mr. . . . uh, Stick."

Randy White was a mess. He puffed his stinking cigarette and paced around his glass-walled office looking at the copy I was turning in. He's a good newspaper editor, but having people in one of his paper's stories getting shot at by people from another story—all while his reporter's house is being ransacked—well, it was a little beyond his experience.

"For pete's sake, Stick, this is Melbourne not Miami. I trust you to do a down-home story on blue crabs, and you've got to come up with a body. And now this."

"It's not as if I planned it, Randy."

"I won't even give you that." He pushed a button on the intercom and handed both stories to the office gofer who appeared seconds later. "Get these in," he said, and the girl disappeared.

"I don't like it one bit. What are you going to do until the cops find Mutt and Jeff?"

"You mean *Mullet* and Jeff? I'm going to stay on the story like any decent reporter would—like you would. I always liked mysteries. Ever read any Dick Francis?"

"If you get yourself killed," Randy said, "I'm going to be real ticked off."

"I'll remember that. You know, Randy, I think *Bonecrack* was one of his best."

"And just what makes you think you'll do any better than the police?"

Randy sort of fell into his high-backed office chair and stared at me across the desk. "You do have it, don't you?"

"A copy of *Bonecrack*? Sure. You want to borrow it?"

"No, you pig-headed gimp! I mean *it!*"

"I don't know what it is you're talking about, Randy."

"The it these thugs are looking for. The it that got Jim Woods killed. Man, I should have figured. Stick, you're going to make me gray before my time."

"You're already gray," I said on my way to the door. "I've gotta run, Randy. I'm meeting two women at a motel down in Jupiter."

"Sure," he said, "that'll be the day; I'll bet you're still saying 'no' to Sam Wagner. Look, Stick, there's just no such thing as perpetual afterglow, and even if there were, I can't see that it would be a substitute for an exceptional string of one-night stands."

So, Randy is a hedonist. I like him anyway. As for me, "That was wonderful. Let's do it again some time" is a worse prospect than doing without. At least on most nights.

When I left him, Randy was frantically searching his hair in the mirror on the file cabinet. All right, so he's also vain. I still like him.

Florida's famous Route 1 runs over five hundred miles, from the Georgia border all the way to Key West. It is far from the quickest way to go north or south, but it's the only way for a tourist to see the Gold Coast at its best. Still, my Camaro likes Interstate 95 much better and can make the two-hour trip from Melbourne to Palm Beach County in an hour and a half on a good day. The prospect of seeing Katie Newman again made this a very good day.

The only trouble with a scenic drive down the interstate is that it gave me too much time to think about Randy's mother hen instincts. The brute brothers were still out there somewhere, they still wanted the disc, and their dispositions probably weren't improving with the passage of time. What would I do if they got to me somehow? Despite the unpleasantness of that prospect, visions of Brer Rabbit came to mind. "Oh, please, Mr. Bad Manz, yuz can burn me with cigarettes, yuz can beat me with a rubber hose, but pleeeeze don't touch my poor legs. Oh, but that would pain me so."

They'd never buy it. What about Katie? The thought of Mullet and Jeff having her alone in a back room somewhere was real nightmare stuff. These guys had been scared off twice now, complete with some nasty job-related injuries, but something told me they would keep coming back, like bad colds. If getting that laser disc was that important, Gene and Edna's Winter Park home wasn't a very good place for Katie to hide out. The police couldn't baby-sit her indefinitely. Maybe Jim's motel. No, too many people at Com-Tech would know about that. I'd have to think on it further.

Who wanted that disc anyway? And why? Jerry Wagner raved about the programming technique, but thus far found nothing suspicious.

"The guy was good," Jerry had said on the phone. "I'll give you that. He sure knows how to maximize efficiency, and I've learned a trick or two, but I haven't seen anything alarming yet. I mean—to die for a communications program, even a great one, seems pretty farfetched."

The whole affair seemed farfetched to me. When I asked him if the programming was revolutionary enough for someone—another industry, or country—to steal and use for their own purposes, he paused before saying "maybe." After he promised to keep working on it, I made a mental note to see Com-Tech's PR man, Dave Bentley, again.

The Riverside Inn is actually on the Jupiter Inlet. Unfortunately, the rocky cove in the motel's backyard is just the kind of place that the worst floating scum always gravitates to, regardless of which way the tides were moving the water through the channel. After a cursory scan of the dead fish, palmetto fronds, and brown foamy unmentionables doing sluggish circles around the man-made shoreline, I turned the car around and parked facing the street.

Moments later, Edna steered the Woods's family station wagon into the motel parking lot. The wood grain decal side panels were badly faded from nearly a decade of Florida sunshine. I watched Mrs. Woods's shoulders rise and fall resignedly as she turned off the ignition and braced herself for the task at hand.

Katie Newman rose from the passenger seat and I nearly missed the transfer into my wheelchair. She wore tight jeans, frayed slightly at the knees, and a gray University of Kansas sweatshirt with its sleeves cut off. The KU Jayhawk was grinning proudly on her chest. Who could blame it? Katie's shoulders, bejeweled with rich brown freckles, stirred some restless inner urgings I never knew I had. Her hair, fiery red in the midmorning sun, was held back by a blue-checkered bandanna that was neatly folded as a headband and tied around her head. Well-worn Reeboks seemed right for her confident, athletic stride. Something told me that the mysterious lady of the black lace dress had a better-than-average jump shot. She probably played a mean game of slow-pitch softball too.

"I told Gene that it wasn't necessary to put you out, Mr. Foster, but he insisted." Edna Woods gave me her version of the patented "men" shrug. Every woman knows it; no two women ever do it quite the same.

"I'm glad he did," I said, trying not to stare past her at the lady who still wore her son's engagement ring. "Call me Stick."

Jim's room was number 107, right next to an ice machine that whined, shuddered, and ka-thunked as if it was on the verge of a massive mechanical breakdown. Edna's hands trembled as she struggled with the key, and after several seconds she bit her lip, passed the key to Katie, and took a deep breath.

"I'm sorry," she said, tears forming in her brown, motherly eyes.

"There's no need to be sorry," Katie said as she held the door open for her almost-mother-in-law.

I could only nod, pondering briefly about the act of selling words for a living . . . especially words about the suffering of others.

I'm not certain what I expected to find there, but unlike my house or Jim's Orlando bungalow, the motel room was neat and tidy. The orange and green flowered bedspread was made up tightly. Clean, unused towels were folded and packed in the stainless-steel wall rack. And new, shrink-wrapped plastic cups were arranged around a squarish brown ice bucket.

I sat in the doorway while Edna and Katie gathered up the

shirts, slacks, and neckties hung in the small closet area and placed them, along with a drawerful of socks, T-shirts, and underwear, in Jim's gray carry-on flight bag. Baby Bear sat on the nightstand, leaning against the telephone. There was a colorful ribbon tied in a bow around his neck, but he looked decidedly lonely to me. On the floor by the same nightstand was a black imitation leather briefcase. While Edna collected Jim's toiletry supplies from the bathroom, and Katie sat on the side of the bed cradling the small stuffed creature in her arms, I wondered whether Jim Woods had left us any clues. I wanted a look in that briefcase, but it seemed a very awkward time to ask.

When Edna left to unlock the car, I offered my lap for the flight bag. Katie hesitated, her moist eyes focused sharply on mine, and then, apparently satisfied, set the suitcase on my knees. She reentered the room, then returned with the briefcase and the bear. I followed her across the parking lot, making little effort not to stare at the back end of her delightfully healthy walk.

"Gene was wondering," Edna said as we approached, "whether Jim might not have left something—you know, helpful—in his briefcase. I told him I wouldn't know what to look for, but he said you might. If you wouldn't mind, Mr. Foster?"

"I was thinking the same thing," I told her, relieved that I hadn't had to ask, and wishing someone would call me Stick. "I'd be glad to have a look, although I'm not sure what to look for either."

Like the motel room, the briefcase held nothing out of the ordinary. Both women looked over my shoulders while I held the open case on my lap and sifted through its well-ordered contents. The pockets in the lid held pencils, pens, and various computer and high-tech journals. In the main compartment, Jim carried a calculator more complicated than any I had ever seen. Next to this work-related tool, was a toy befitting the dead man I was slowly coming to know. It was a miniaturized chess computer, undoubtedly state-of-the-art.

Separating these supermachines from the bottom of the briefcase was a yellow legal pad. Even before I could pull it out, I knew that both of the women behind me were crying. The first sheet of green-lined paper was the only one in the pad with anything on it at all. It was largely covered with notes and doodles—predominant among them the name "Katie," surrounded by hearts and several sketchy caricatures of a stuffed bear.

$\triangledown$

7

I POCKETED THE NOTEPAD'S top sheet, and when emotions were once again manageable, I invited the women to be my guests for an early lunch. They both looked like declining, but I made it clear that I was still concerned about Katie's safety and needed to talk to them about minimizing the risk until the two mystery men were caught. Captain Toby's, I explained, was just up the road, in Stuart—best seafood for miles. In the end, I won them over, and Edna pulled out behind me and followed my blue Camaro up the coast, to the restaurant by the St. Lucie Inlet.

"Jimmy didn't like seafood," Edna said. She stared at the seafloor waterscape imbedded in the wooden tabletop.

Katie watched a fishing boat move toward us, chugging slowly through the inlet from the Atlantic. It was clear that neither woman was about to tackle the menu, so I ordered chowder and fresh shrimp cocktail all around.

"Have you ever gone out on a charter?" Katie asked, indicating the string of docks bearing advertisements for day and/or night fishing trips.

"Sure," I said. "I go whenever I can, back up north. I did

a story on the *Miss Cape Canaveral* two years ago. Her crew is the best; the wheelchair doesn't bother them a bit. Their boat can handle about sixty people at a time, and it's sure pretty out there on a day like this. Getting out of sight of land is a little scary the first time, but the captain knows the coastal waters better than you and I know our bathtubs."

I almost drew smiles, but not quite. It just wasn't the time yet.

"About tonight," I injected into the silence that followed, "I don't think Katie should stay at your place, Mrs. Woods." There may have been a flicker of relief in both sets of eyes, but it was carefully covered. "I'm sure the police are doing everything they can," I said, looking at Katie. "But as long as those thugs are on the loose, there's no sense advertising where you're staying. Anyway, if they came after you again, you'd be bringing more trouble on Mr. and Mrs. Woods."

Edna started to object, but Katie placed her hand over that of the older woman and nodded her head. "I've thought about that," she said. "Perhaps a motel. A cheap one. I don't want to go home yet, not if there's a chance that I can help find out what happened. After all, I asked you to help me. I want to *do* something."

"I've been thinking," I said as inspiration struck just in time, "I'd like to call a friend in Orlando. She lives alone, mostly, and has an extra room. Would you consider staying there for a few days?"

Edna reluctantly headed back toward the Florida State Turnpike and Orlando, leaving Katie in my care. I told her we would be by for Katie's things sometime after supper.

"I've never gotten to park in one of these spots," Katie said as we backed out of the restaurant lot.

"It's kind of mind boggling," I said, "having my portrait painted on parking spaces like this all over Florida. Why I've heard they're now doing me coast-to-coast. I try not to let it go to my head, but it is a good likeness, don't you think?"

Now she was smiling. If I had had any feeling in my knees, I just know they would have felt mushy. I read a story off the wire once about some experimental muscle control testing being done with certain shades of the color red. When the hue was just right, the report said, and the person being tested had to stare at a cardboard placard painted with the stuff, he would experience a measurable loss of strength, finding himself unable to lift objects he had hoisted easily only moments before. Whether it was Katie's hair, her eyes, or the freckles, I was glad I didn't have to lift anything just then. I hung on to the wheel and sped north.

On the way, I called Sam Wagner and Dave Bentley. Sam said that while she'd rather I stay over for a few days, she would be glad to help Katie out.

Dave Bentley sounded uneasy on the phone but agreed to meet me in the employee parking area.

When we checked in and pulled through the employees' guard gate at the cape, we found Dave pacing near a blue and white pin-striped, short-bed pickup. He had a sandwich in his hand, and his lunch bag and thermos sat on the truck's hood. I steered the rusty Z28 into the vacant spot beside him, and he looked around nervously, then squatted next to my window. He recoiled physically when he saw Katie.

"Dave, you've met Katie Newman, I think. Are you all right?"

"Maybe we should talk in private," he said, his eyes darting toward Katie, but never really landing squarely. "I mean, it's all very touchy and I know it must be difficult for Miss Newman this soon after—"

"I'm quite capable of dealing with the truth, Mr. Bentley. Jim always said you were a straightforward guy. I want you to be straightforward with me. What's going on here?"

"Can we go someplace else to talk, at least," Dave said, frowning at my wheelchair. "I don't have a backseat either." He jerked his thumb at the pickup.

"My backseat is stored in the carport," I told him, "but you can hunker back there if you don't mind sitting on the floor." The carpet I'd installed to cover the exposed metal where the seat had been was sandy, but better than the bed of his truck. "Where do you want to go?"

"Anywhere," Dave said, climbing in next to my chair and trying to get comfortable. "There's a picnic area over on the Banana River."

The sunny recreational area bordered by the Banana River—as that part of the Intercoastal Waterway is called—was dotted with tourists and locals, and there were scenic, palm-tree-shaded picnic tables everywhere.

"Jim liked this place," Katie said as I pulled to a stop along a rock-lined section of the Atlantic shoreline, let Dave Bentley get out of the back, and retrieved, unfolded, and climbed aboard my chair.

We sat for a time in silence at a well-monogrammed picnic table, letting the warm sea breeze speak to us of faraway places.

"What's up, Dave?" I said at last. "You don't look so good."

"There are rumors," he said slowly, glancing uncomfortably at Katie again. "Bad ones, about Jim."

Katie stiffened, but remained silent, looking out to sea.

"I mean there are guys in suits asking a lot of questions around work. CIA or FBI. Or so we're told. The word is"—he paused again, shaking his head—"I mean, I don't believe it or anything, but they're saying Jim might have been trying to sell out stuff—like to the Russians or something—and maybe he double-crossed them. I'm sorry, Katie."

Katie rose, and the back of her neck was deep red, but she said nothing. Instead, she started throwing pieces of seashell into the rolling waves. What a sidearm.

"Dave," I said, "why would they say that? What would make them suspect Jim Woods of something like that?"

"He was always modifying his computer. Every kind of add-on he could find. Well, it seems he had some gadget rigged to his terminal—a laser dealy or some such, real high-tech. Anyway, it's gone now, but somebody saw him using it to copy data off our system. These guys in suits are real concerned."

"Who saw him, Dave?" I asked. Katie turned her green eyes on the public relations man and he looked helpless under her gaze.

"I don't know."

"Then find out," Katie said.

Yes, ma'am.

$\triangledown$

8

KATIE NEWMAN CRADLED BUTKIS in the crook of one arm, stroking his soft brown coat while she surveyed my ravaged home.

"Jim's place was worse," she said, following me into the bedroom. "But what do you think they want?"

"This," I said, turning my chair sideways to the nightstand and removing a yellow box from the bottom drawer.

"Preparation H?" Katie said, the freckles on her nose bunching up in distaste.

I rummaged through the carton and handed her Jim's wallet. "No," I said, enjoying the look on her face. "I meant this."

I explained about the laser disc and Sam's brother at Morton. "The wallet should go to his folks," I said, "and the disc belongs to Com-Tech, but I think I'll keep it for a while longer."

When it occurred to me that Katie was looking for her photograph in the salt-stiffened billfold, I fought a surge of embarrassment before explaining why it was no longer there. I thought momentarily about making up something, but found that I really wanted her to know. I also told her why the picture was no longer pinned up in my office. If the first

41

admission amused her, the second sobered her immediately. "I'm sorry" was all I could say. Katie smiled and said it was okay. I hoped she was right, but thought I saw something in her face that said it concerned her far more than she was letting on.

It occurred to me—though I can't put my finger on just why—that someone had been in my office since the break-in the previous afternoon. Everything seemed to be where I had left it, but it felt wrong somehow. I recalled Dave Bentley's face when he had said "CIA" and was having that same distasteful feeling myself. I'd always wondered what real paranoia felt like. Knowing now didn't help; I could neither appreciate it, nor think it away. In my heart, I *knew* my house was bugged, and I hated myself for being so sure. I wasn't real pleased about the explanations I had just sung to Katie. And who knows who else.

The disc obviously could not go back with the Preparation H, but I couldn't imagine any safe place at the moment. It felt like a hot coal on my lap. In my spooked imagination, I heard it calling out to those who wanted to take it away from me: "Here I am! In here with the stupid crippled guy!"

"What's the matter?"

Katie's voice brought me down. Almost. I raised the back of my hand to my forehead and found that I was sweating.

"Oh, sorry," I said, reaching for my scratch pad. "It's nothing."

Even as I scribbled my fears out on the paper, I felt patently foolish and dead certain—both in equal measures. Apparently Katie had no qualms about believing me. She nodded her head and pointed to the far wall of my office.

"Is that the chair you want?"

"Yes, thank you," I said, silently mouthing the word "Fast!"

"Just throw it in the trunk. I'll bring the wheels." I watched Katie pick up the rigid frame, ultralight alloy sports chair and carry it down the hall. While I balanced the pop-off wheels across my toes, I searched frantically for a place to hide the laser disc. As I followed Katie through the kitchen, decidedly distracted, I smelled the acrid odor of a household job left undone in all the turmoil. It came, as always, from the laundry room.

"Meet you in the car," I said, turning aside.

Despite my love for Butkis T. Cat, I hate cleaning out his litter box.

The steel-gray sedan was a good block behind us, but I'd seen enough *Rockford Files* reruns to know a tail when I saw one. Running from Mullet and Jeff was natural enough, but these guys in three-piece suits were supposed to be the white hats. So why did I want so desperately to lose them? Maybe I didn't like the conclusions they were coming to. Maybe I wanted to find the truth for Katie. Maybe it was getting personal.

I tried speeding up, but they held their position. After two unsignaled turns and a nice move down a narrow alley, I was sure I had lost them. I was wrong. In fact, now that they knew that I knew, it seemed the game was up. The white hats were no longer shadowing us; they were chasing us.

"Hang on, Katie," I said, putting the hand-controlled peddle to the floor. "I probably shouldn't let go of anything just now, so how about if you help me call in some reinforcements?"

"What's the number?" Katie asked stoutly, glancing over her freckled shoulder at the full-bore Chrysler coming on fast. The Jayhawk was still grinning. Dumb, crazy, lucky bird.

I recited the number and had Katie hold the phone to my ear when she was finished dialing.

"Rita? This is Stick Foster. Can you patch me through to the Fonze? It's an emergency. Thanks."

After what seemed like several long and harrowing moments, Officer Sanchez's firm voice crackled through the car phone.

"What's up, Stick?"

"They're on my tail, Fonze. I've got Katie Newman with me. They must want her bad."

"Mr. Stilles's friends? Where are you, Stick?"

"I'm on Shorecrest, but you say where and I'll bring 'em to you."

He must have heard the screeching tires.

"How fast are you going?"

"Too fast," I said. "Where are you?"

Once he told me, I started feeling better. If it hadn't been for the various and sundry Melbourne pedestrians, the rest might have been fun. Still, when the Fonze—lights and sirens going full tilt—came shooting out of the Sun Bank parking lot, I had to laugh. He missed my rear bumper by a couple of feet and locked up his brakes just in time to watch the white hats destroy his cruiser's passenger door. The rest of the force were on them like a pack of wolves, but Katie and I were already on our way to Orlando. Somehow, I was pretty sure that I had just called in my last favor from Melbourne's finest.

"Nice job, Fonze!" I said into my car phone. But he didn't hear me because his radio microphone must have been locked "on" in his fist while he got the bad news from the feds. I've often wondered whether that kind of swearing is a mandatory part of marine basic training. When he returned his attention to the open line between us, I had to hold the receiver away from my ear until he had settled himself some. Katie just smiled and waited with me.

"Oh, really?" I said when there was a break long enough. "You mean it wasn't Mullet and Jeff? It was who? The FBI? Why ever would the FBI be chasing me?"

Officer Sanchez was insistent that we drag a certain part

of our lower anatomy back to the police station on the double, but I guess I must have chosen to lose the signal somewhere about then because I hung up.

My car phone rang all the way to Conway. The Fonze finally gave up and I drove north through the south Orlando suburb. If he guessed where I was going, he might even call the OPD. Maybe I should have called him back. Nah. I did call Jerry Wagner's office to warn him about the white hats, but he'd already left for the day. Leaving a message didn't seem like a good idea either, so I decided to try phoning his home when I got to the gym.

Phil was juggling wrenches, and the folks at Melbourne Ford, where he works from noon to nine at night, frown on personal calls, but warning him about the FBI seemed like an important enough reason to interrupt somebody's valve job.

"Your hands are dirty," I said when Phil came on the line.

He laughed. "Okay, Sherlock, what's up?"

"You're going to have some visitors. In suits."

"You mean the FBI?"

"They've already been there?" I said.

"This morning, at the docks. I didn't tell 'em a thing."

"Well, don't be surprised if they come back. My house is bugged and they heard me talking to Katie about the . . . ah . . . Preparation H. They think Jim Woods was the bad guy, and until I can prove he wasn't, I'd like to hang on to Propjob's little gift. Try to stay out of their way, will you?"

"Sure, but where will you be?"

"Maybe it's better you don't know, Phil."

"All right, Sherlock. Watch your backside!"

I hung up when he started humming "Ring of Fire."

The old Armory gym sits just off Highway 50, south of the Fashion Square Mall in east Orlando—just a block from the Fresh Hot doughnut shop. It's worth a drive over from the coast just to watch the doughnuts ride up the conveyor belt from the fryer before you eat them. Fresh Hot doughnuts really do melt in your mouth. The Orange Wheels often practice at the Armory, at least whenever there isn't an air-conditioned gymnasium available for free.

After introducing Katie to Sam and the other team members already present, and getting Jerry's home number, I rolled to the lobby and used the pay phone. Busy. I'd try again after practice. From the doorway, I watched Katie and Sam get acquainted over warm-up shots from the field. Katie's jumper was clean and sharp while Sam's roll-away set shot looked deceptively underpowered, until it dropped in without touching the rim.

As they sized each other up, the friendly chitchat and the casual hoop show began to grow a little too intense. The warm-up was turning into a full-scale one-on-one confrontation.

"Pretty competitive. Couldn't we break her legs or something?" said Joe Stetler, rolling up with a big grin on his dark face. "With those two on the court at once, nobody'd notice me at all. I'd be the league's high scorer in no time."

Joe is a double amputee with arms like Phil Stilles's. His black hair is receding, so he looks to be in his forties—a difficult cross to bear for an athletic man of thirty-five. "Legs are one thing," he'd bemoaned in private moments, "but my *hair*? Why do I have to lose my hair?" Stet had been the Wheels' player-coach for two years, and he regularly dropped in three pointers, almost at will. I've seen him hit from half court on more than one occasion.

"I don't know which one of them is more beautiful," I confessed. "Is that too chauvinistic for a modern, sensitive-kind-of-guy to say?"

"I don't know, Stick, but it's sure enough the truth. Too bad about the lady's fiancé. Sam told us what you're working on. I hope you come up with something."

"Thanks, Stet."

Katie's fake was smooth and fast. She drove for the basket, clearly intending to leave Sam and her orange sports chair turning the wrong way in a swirl of dust. She couldn't have known that Sam's reverse move was one of the best in the league. She couldn't have known just how fast an ultralight alloy chair can spin 180 degrees. She found out the hard way. The wheelchair spun like a whirlwind, its foot rests catching Katie's ankles, sending her sprawling headlong across the key. Sam stroked again, slapped the loose basketball against her left handrim, let it ride up to her as the wheel rolled forward, and laid it up and in for two points . . . without ever looking back.

"You think I should break this up before there's bloodshed?" Stet asked with a grin.

"I guess so," I said, uncomfortable with the tension that radiated from the women like Florida sun off a black tar roof.

"Okay, now, let's see what kind of shape you're in!"

▽

9

ALL RIGHT, SO I'M not in the best of shape anymore. My outside shot would have been lots better, though, if it hadn't been for all the forward and backward wind sprints before practice. Sometimes I think Stet must have been a drill sergeant instead of a disillusioned first louie. He never talks much about Nam, but on those occasions when I've worked out with the Orlando Orange Wheels, I've been ready to swear he was taking it all out on us. Except that everybody else seems to enjoy it.

Grabbing the pay phone receiver reminded me of another punishment for shirking regular workouts. The skin on my palms was burning hot. My "everyday" calluses just couldn't hold up to a full court press; I would have a fine set of blisters to show for my efforts.

"Hello?" It must have been Meghan Wagner's voice, but she sounded almost frantic.

"Mrs. Wagner? This is Stick Foster. Is Jerry home?"

"You! How dare you drag Jerry into your ugly business? If they hurt him, I'll see you in—"

"Mrs. Wagner, please! If who hurts him? Where's Jerry now?" There was something odd about her tone, but then she was scared and angry.

"They took him. He was just getting out of the car. What have you gotten him into?" Her voice rose almost to a screech, shrill but forced, almost as if she were reading from a "B" movie script.

"I'm sorry. I didn't think I was getting him into anything, but I am very sorry. Have you called the police?"

"They just left." Some of the fury abated, but the strange hostility remained.

"What did they look like?" I asked, though all white hats looked the same, at least on television.

"A small man and a tall one with dark hair. Something was wrong with his face. Who are they, Mr. Foster, and why did they take Jerry? I want some answers from somebody."

I was too stunned to answer, even if I'd had an answer to give. How could Mullet and Jeff have known about Jerry? Even where he lived? If the white hats were watching and bugging my house, how could the thug brothers have heard my conversation with Katie? I couldn't even remember mentioning Jerry. The sensation was not unlike a bad round of "knock" poker. You get this confident feeling after rapping your knuckles on the table and hearing the groans of the others around you when you lay down your straight flush. The sick, gut-wrenching ache comes suddenly when the player across from you lays down a royal flush.

I was wondering whether I could afford to re-ante up my share of the pot, when Meghan Wagner interrupted my waking nightmare.

"Mr. Foster? Are you still there?"

"Yes."

"Look. I'm sorry," she said heavily. "I need anybody's help who can give it. Please help Jerry if you can. Where are you, anyway?"

Telling Jerry's wife that these men had torn up two homes and shot one of my friends was out of the question, as was telling her where I was. But she needed to be talked to and I was too rattled to do her any good. "Just a second, Mrs. Wagner. I'm getting Sam. She'll tell you what she can, and I'll try to find out where they've taken Jerry. I'll do everything I can."

It sounded as feeble to me as it must have to Meghan Wagner, but there was nothing for it. I spoke briefly to Katie and Sam, telling them I had changed my mind about leaving Katie at Sam's, sent Sam to talk with her sister-in-law on the phone, and then got Joe Stetler off to the side. Katie followed me as the rest of the team packed up to leave.

"Stet? Do you still carry a handgun?"

"Of course," he said. "I tote more jewelry around in a day than you'll handle in your lifetime. They think that nobody would suspect a black gimp of hauling diamonds and such—it's a 'secret' racist joke in the head office—but the job pays good, and I enjoy it, and someday I might just disappear with a couple million dollars worth of rocks! But until then, I don't take any chances."

Joe Stetler's exact responsibilities at Hales Fine Jewelry chain have never been quite clear to me, but he is apparently something like an economy version of a Brinks truck.

"I need to borrow it, Joe. Or something else. This ComTech thing is getting way out of hand. They've just snatched Sam's brother—right in front of his house—and they're still after Katie and me. I don't run as well as I used to, so in case I have to stand and fight . . ."

"Sure, Stick. Come on."

Out in the darkening lot, Joe reached under the driver's seat of his black '86 Monte Carlo SS and produced a shoulder rigged, automatic pistol. Two extra clip holders were full and taped to the harness.

"It's a Browning 9mm auto," he said, pulling it free and pointing out the safety. "Fourteen shots, then it locks open. Hit this release and the empty clip will drop right out. Slam the new clip home and release the slide, here. You ever shot a pistol?"

"Phil Stilles's .357, once," I said, "and a .45 in the army. Once or twice."

"This won't jump so much, won't be quite as loud, but you'll have eight more shots than the Magnum and a heck of a faster reload. Don't even show it unless you're dead sure you can pull the trigger—a hair trigger by the way. Also, the 9mm is an extremely high velocity round. At close range it can go clean through a person's body and come out the other side. Be careful."

He hopped into the front seat of his classic Chevy and flipped over the corduroy-covered, one-inch foam cushion he had been sitting on throughout practice. On the underside, totally unnoticed until now, was a smaller weapon, quite unlike the Browning. The sound of crackling Velcro echoed in the oak-fringed parking lot as he pulled it free and broke it open on its hinges.

"This is a two-shot derringer," Joe said to Katie. "It breaks open like this and is chambered for the same round as the Browning. It's a little harder to hang on to, and you can't really aim it. Just flick off the safety, point, and shoot. The trigger automatically resets after the first shot, so you can squeeze off both rounds, one right after the other."

If Katie was put off by the idea of carrying a gun, she sure didn't let on. After sliding the weapon into her back right pocket, she leaned into the Monte and kissed Joe on the cheek.

"Thanks, Stet," she said. "I'll return it soon, unfired I hope."

"Here," Joe said, handing me a third-full box of 9mm ammunition. "If you need this, you're in real hot water, but my backup is a .38 special, so you might as well have the rest of the box with you. Watch yourself, okay?"

"I will, Stet. And maybe somebody should keep one eye on Sam?"

"Gladly!"

"Thanks."

* * *

I drove around Gene and Edna Woods's block three times before stopping at the curb in front of their house. The eerie glow of the color television illuminated their living room curtains, and the front porch lights lit most of the yard. I backed reluctantly into their driveway, but left the motor running. Joe's shoulder holster felt awkward under my white *Sun Coaster* windbreaker, and the weight of the pistol pushed back hard against the thumping of my heart.

"Be careful," I said to Katie. "Peek in the window, see if everything looks right before you ring the bell."

"If everything is status quo," Katie whispered, looking at her watch and forcing a smile, "they should be watching Vanna. I don't know what they see in *Wheel of Fortune* . . . and I'll never understand why people buy vowels."

Gripping the derringer in her hand, she slipped out of the passenger seat and walked up the porch steps to the front door. This was one of those times when I missed my legs most. I was never exactly a Rambo sort of guy. But, while my father taught me to avoid fights whenever possible, he also made it clear to me that it was wrong to sit by and watch somebody else take an unfair beating. The tricks he passed on, added to what I learned in the army, had come in handy on several occasions. Now, knowing that if anything went wrong inside that house, I would be helpless to intervene, I turned to prayer. My father taught me that too.

Fortunately—or providentially, as the case may be— nothing was amiss at the Woodses' home. Though it seemed to take much too long, Gene answered the door, hugged Katie enthusiastically, and ushered her inside, explaining that someone named Rosemary was about to solve the puzzle. I turned off the engine and breathed a well-deserved sigh of relief.

I called the Orlando police and a deputy friend with the Orange County sheriff's department, but if there were any leads on Jerry Wagner, nobody was talking. I dialed Meghan Wagner's number with no small trepidation, but it couldn't be helped. In my initial shock, it hadn't occurred to me to ask about the car Mullet and Jeff were driving. The police probably had, but as a reporter I felt it was something I should do myself. She described the burnt orange, late seventies Riviera with only a hole where the trunk lock should have been and then gave me Trish Taylor's unlisted home number and wrote down my car phone number, promising to give it to the men who had Jerry—if they called.

"Tell them I'll trade what they want for Jerry," I told her, trying to sound confident. "And," I added, thinking of numerous television and movie screenplays, "listen for any background noises that might give us a clue to where they're calling from."

"That's what the police said," Meghan told me. "They even hooked up a tape recorder to the phone."

"Oh. Well, how about rewinding it when we're done. If the police get what these thugs want from me—and they want it too—we won't be able to trade it for Jerry. Do you understand that?"

"Yes. I understand."

I hung up and called Todd Gulick, a junior reporter for the *Sun Coaster*. He wouldn't like my interrupting his nightly time with Vanna, but it couldn't be helped. He was the only certified Stick Foster impersonator at the paper, and if there was going to be a Shore Line column in the morning, he was going to have to get started on it.

I filled him in on the kidnapping and the misguided attempt to shift suspicion onto the dead computer specialist, putting special emphasis on the implication that certain official law enforcement agencies were spending the good citizens' tax dollars chasing reporters instead of criminals. Todd, though his sense of humor needs serious work, has more subtlety than I do, so I felt confident this last point would be well made. When he was comfortable with what I wanted, I let him go.

With his white shirts and horn-rimmed glasses, Todd needed only a pocket pencil protector to fill out the stereotypical nerd look. Everyone knew why his prospects were limited to the bespectacled local librarian, but I had impulsively promised to help him rectify that.

$\triangledown$

10

WHEN KATIE RETURNED TO the car, her own flight bag across her shoulder, she was chuckling to herself. Seeing the question on my face she cocked her thumb toward the Woods's front room.

"You'll be glad to know, Stick, that a bimbo named Rosemary just blew nineteen hundred bucks on a brass bedroom set, a Styrofoam sailboat, and a digital bathroom scale that talks!"

"Sorry I missed that," I said, loving the way she said "Stick." Katie was an amazing piece of work. She was gorgeous, of course, but she was so much more: intelligent, tough, funny, sometimes straightforward, and, sometimes, very mysterious. She could be so dead serious it was scary, yet her laughter could make a top-notch journalist turn in his press pass for a poet's quill pen. Fortunately, I'm not that good a journalist . . . yet.

Katie had showered. I never realized that my poor Camaro could smell like a field of spring flowers. Her hair was still wet, brushed back and tied with a piece of black and red ribbon. The clean white sweatshirt, its long sleeves pushed up on her forearms, sported the same grinning Jayhawk, but boasted KU's 1988 NCAA National Basketball Championship victory. I had to admit that Danny Manning had been one of the best college players in a lot of years; the Clippers were lucky to get him. And Larry Brown was, both at KU and San Antonio, a fine coach. But it was so demeaning for me, being jealous of a cartoon bird with yellow clown shoes.

"By the way," I said, trying not to roll my eyes when I breathed in, "keep a lookout for a late seventies orange Riviera with no trunk lock."

"It'll be a step up from watching Vanna!"

Oh, that smile.

After circling the block several times, driving out through Maitland and Goldenrod, then skirting Winter Park on my way back into Orlando proper, I was finally satisfied that we weren't being followed. Relaxing at least enough to stop watching the rearview mirror, I called Trish Taylor. She wasn't at all pleased when I told her about Jerry and the thug brothers.

"What will they do to him?"

"Nothing, I hope." I didn't sound as confident as I had wanted to. "At least I think what they really want is the disc. That's why I called. Before I trade it to them or lose it to the FBI, or who knows, I wanted to find out what you've discovered. Anything?"

"Not really."

"Nothing? I mean everything on that disc is routine?"

"I've looked at some of the programming, Mr. Foster. It's just not that big a deal. Oh sure, the parallel processing is most impressive, innovative in fact, but bugging people's homes, shooting and kidnapping, it's not that good."

"I've been thinking about that. Look, call me Stick. This program, the one on the disc, wouldn't it be a permanent part of Com-Tech's NASA-related software?"

"Sure. Mr. Woods may have copied it to the laser disc, but the operating original would still be on-line at Com-Tech.

Probably a ROM chip. You know, Read Only Memory. Even though he could have copied it out to the disc, he couldn't have removed or replaced all the backups without having had new plug-in chips designed and installed."

"So," I said, "there must be something about this disc that they want. Any idea what that might be?"

"Sorry. None."

I gave her my number and hung up. Katie was not satisfied.

"Look," she said, her green eyes insistent in the light of oncoming traffic, "if Jimmy said he 'discovered something wrong,' then he did. We've just got to find out what it is."

"Jerry Wagner was trying," I said carefully. "Now he's in the same jam Jim was in. Getting him out of it before he dies too has to come first."

"Of course," Katie said. "I'm sorry. I didn't mean it to sound like that."

"I know."

Hiding out with Katie Newman wasn't going to be easy. After all, she had her luggage. All I had was an extra wheelchair. While I drove north toward Altamonte Springs, I wondered if she'd loan me her razor so I could trim my beard. I figured the toothbrush was definitely out of the question. In the end, I pulled into the Kartman's Discount Department Store near the jai alai fronton and picked up a couple changes of clothes and some of life's more necessary paraphernalia. I was very glad for plastic money and wondered idly how I'd finagle the cost onto my expense account.

Altamonte's La Conche Grande Motor Lodge, with all its southern charm, belongs to Hector Heeta—an old high school classmate who is well connected in "certain" Latin circles. Peeling pink paint barely covers the long stucco building, and a plethora of long-broken conch shells line the driveway and the parking lot.

Inside the small rooms, dusty curtains and dirty terrazzo floors are overseen by a host of semidomesticated cockroaches. Hector's mother is the sole housekeeper, and who would dare complain about a seventy-year-old Puerto Rican woman to her youngest son?

"Buenos noches, my old amigo," Hector said, putting down the greyhound racing form and stepping up to the counter. He looked past me, obviously at the passenger out in my Camaro, and whistled.

"Good work, Nicholas," he said approvingly, his right eyebrow rising higher than the left. "And it's about time too."

There was no sense asking Hector to call me Stick. He'd called me by my given name since we ran together in high school. He had pretty fixed ideas on nicknames, and nobody ever called him Hec—at least not more than once.

"It's not what you think, Hector."

"Of course not. But for you, the first hour is free!"

If Katie noticed the pre-Hoover, post-fifties motif of the motel room, she sure didn't let on. Instead, she grabbed some things from her flight bag and took first dibs on the bathroom. She returned wearing black silk jogging shorts and a long, red, loose-fitting sleeveless T-shirt. The sounds of a desperate, cheering crowd—emanating from the dog track next door—drifted in through the screened window, but I hardly noticed. I decided to take a cold shower.

"I've been thinking," Katie said when I emerged from the bathroom, forcing my chair through the narrow door, "what if they don't call Jerry's wife and, consequently, don't call you to talk trade?"

"That's not a very pleasant prospect," I said, checking the AC adapter plug on the portable car phone before pulling back the faded spread on my bed. Katie sat cross-legged on the other, just as if we were chatting in Lake Eola Park.

"They might just do him like they did Jimmy, you know,

when and if they believe he doesn't have what they want."

"I thought of that too," I confessed, "but right now Meghan is our only link." I glanced at the bedside stand bolted to the wall between us. With the amount of firepower and sophisticated communication equipment piled there, someone might easily take us for a high-tech, modern version of Bonnie and Clyde.

"Not really," Katie said. "There is another way to find out where they've taken him."

I had the sudden impression that I didn't want to know what the other way was. But Katie was going to tell me anyway.

"They want the disc, right? They're sure we have it. They're getting information from someone, or they're bugging your house themselves. Am I right so far?"

I nodded. "I guess so." The word *formidable* was really right on the mark. My first instincts are pretty amazing sometimes.

"So," she went on, confidence rising, "what if we fed them some information? Let's say that you were to let on that I knew where you'd hidden the disc—maybe even give it to me—then say you were to leave me at your house, just for a few minutes? Do you see?"

She was grinning like the cursed Jayhawk on her T-shirt; didn't she go anywhere without that blasted bird? I must have looked as stupid as I felt, shocked by the ramifications of Katie's suggestion.

"I'm right," she said, taking my silence to mean a lack of suitable objection. "All you have to do then is follow them to wherever they take me and call the police!"

All I had to do . . . good grief. She was formidable all right. And mad as a hatter.

After I convinced her that we might at least give the thug brothers a chance to call, and Hector a chance to check his sources before trying to storm the unknown castle, Katie finally mellowed out enough to switch off the lights and go to bed. "Think about it," she insisted, "okay?"

I promised I would.

"Tell me how you ended up . . . in a chair," Katie asked after a moment's silence.

"Fell off the garage roof," I answered, knowing she would be disappointed.

"You sure adjusted well. Is life much different afterward? I mean besides not being able to walk?"

"Life is totally different," I said, glad to be in the dark end of the room watching Katie's profile silhouetted against the window curtains by the lights of the taco stand across the parking lot.

"What do you mean?" she said, slipping out of her T-shirt and shorts before nestling under the covers.

"Well," I answered, after I'd caught my breath, "it's like starting over. Like being a different person altogether."

"In what way? *You* don't change."

"Oh, you don't lose the use of your legs without changing some, but I just meant that most of your friends treat you like someone different. They cast in their lots with a tall athletic guy they could talk to eye to eye . . . not a crippled-up man the same height as their nieces and nephews. And wheelchairs make many able-bodied people real uncomfortable, like being around someone with cancer or AIDS. They know, intellectually, that they can't get those diseases or have their legs collapse underneath them by being friendly and treating the person like a human being, but maybe just the thought *what if* makes some people act like that."

"Hector doesn't seem that way."

"Hector knows all about discrimination."

"I take it you lost some friends."

"I lost a fiancée too."

The small motel room remained quiet for several moments before Katie said, "I'm sorry."

"Of all people," I said, trying to put a smile back in my voice, "*you* don't need to be sorry. And there's a good side too: I've made better friends since. What I miss most is walking into somebody's house, grabbing a Pepsi out of the refrigerator, and sitting down to watch TV until they come home from work."

"I don't get it," Katie said. "Why can't you do that now?"

"Why didn't I just march into Gene and Edna's with you?"

"Oh . . ."

"Oh, indeed," I said with a chuckle. "I don't mind being carried up and down stairs . . . as long as the people doing it aren't apt to hurt themselves. It's not a pride or dignity thing with me, but having the right and the ability to 'just drop in' is a special part of friendship that I never thought much about . . . until I couldn't do it anymore. The first Spanish phrase Hector ever taught me was: '*Mi casa es su casa.*' My house is your house. But I can't even get in his *casa* by myself anymore!"

"I'd never have thought about that."

"Nobody ever does. Well, nobody but Phil Stilles. I never mentioned anything about this to him, but the day after I met him, he went home and built me a ramp into his house. Not a back porch job either; he put it right smack up to the front door."

"He must be quite a guy."

"The best."

$\triangledown$

11

Wʜᴇɴ ᴛʜᴇ sᴏꜰᴛ ᴋɴᴏᴄᴋɪɴɢ woke me from dreams wonderful beyond description, Katie had already pulled on her T-
shirt—inside out—and was pointing the derringer at the door.

"Nicholas! *Mi amigo!* It's me. Hector. I have some news
for you."

I pulled the Browning from its holster, steadied it across
the seat back of the wheelchair I'd left parked between the
beds, and motioned Katie to unlock the door and cover me
from the bathroom.

"Come in," I said unsteadily, praying that Hector was
alone, not being forced to lead someone to us.

When his grinning face appeared in the doorway, I nearly
blew his head clean off. All right, so I was a little tense. Anyway, the cellular phone at my elbow rang at just that moment, causing me to come six inches up off the bed,
squeezing hard on the automatic's hair trigger in the process.
Hector saw the gun, and the startled look on my face, and
fell to the floor petitioning all deity in rapid-fire Spanish.
Fortunately, I had forgotten about the gun's safety, and no
amount of adrenaline could have persuaded the deadly
weapon to fire.

"It's all right, Hector!" I shouted, prying my white knuckles off the pistol and trying to breathe normally. "I'm sorry, really. It's just the phone. It caught me off guard."

While Hector closed the door behind him and bilingually cursed several generations of my family, I picked up the phone, only to be cursed out by my boss, Randy White.

"Confound you, Stick! What are you trying to do to me?" he yelled into my ear while Hector paused long enough to pick Katie's black silk jogging shorts up off the floor. "There's a major gimp hunt going on here, and guess who the gimp is? I've got the cops, the water patrol, the FBI, and who-knows-who-else in my face this morning. I don't know exactly what you did to piss them all off, but you'd better get your butt in here and straighten all this out. Do you hear me?"

"Loud and clear, boss," I said, motioning for Hector to leave Katie's clothing alone. "Look, you're upset. Why don't we talk later. How about lunch sometime?"

"Don't how-about-lunch me, Foster! I'll drag your . . . Where are you anyway?"

"I'd rather not say just now," I told him. Sounds of a shower came from the bathroom, and Hector sat down on the foot of Katie's bed and watched the door with great interest.

"But this story is getting bigger all the time, chief. Why, I wouldn't be surprised if this scoop puts the *Melbourne Sun Coaster* on the map, right up there with the *Times* and the *Trib*! This could very well move you up, Randy."

"You think so? What have you got?"

"Well, one of my most reliable sources, a man of considerable influence I might add, has just arrived. Tell Todd to stand by the phone. I'll get back to you as soon as I can."

"Stick! Wait a min—"

I didn't hear the rest because I hung up.

Hector laughed. "Nicholas, you are so full of crap. I have

always wondered how you Protestants can sling such bull. At least I can go to confession after I, ah, shade the truth."

"Who's shading the truth? Aren't you everything I said, and more?"

"Well . . ."

"There you are."

We both turned toward the squeaky bathroom door in time to see Katie's freckled arm reach out and point to the silk shorts on her bed.

"Do you think that she wants these, amigo?" Hector grinned fiendishly.

"Yes, Hector. I think that's exactly what she wants. She is Katie Newman," I said, pointing back toward the bathroom, "and I think you'd better do as she asks . . . pronto!"

Hector looked back, right down the twin barrels of Katie's 9mm handgun. Without a word, his grin all but gone, Hector hung the black shorts gingerly on the derringer's front sights and watched them disappear back through the door.

"A guy could get killed around here," Hector whispered.

"One already has," I said, nodding at the bathroom while I hopped into my wheelchair. "Katie was going to marry him this Christmas."

Only after more formal introductions—accompanied by admiring stares and suggestive glances from Hector—was I able to extract the information my friend had gathered. Some local gang members had located the abandoned orange Riviera, but there was no sign of Mullet and Jeff.

"If they are hole up with a nab in this town, amigo," Hector insisted, "my friends would probably know it. No, I see it like this: your buddies stole the Riviera, snatched the Morton Manufacturing guy, ditched the old wheels, picked up some new wheels—maybe their own—and headed back to the coast. That is where it is going down, Nicholas.

"My cousin, Roberto, says that times are looking heavy from Titusville all the way to Melbourne. All sorts of new people are hanging around the cape—and they are not all tourists. What with the *federales*, Senator Holcum, and the antispace demonstrations, and the coming *Discovery* launch, there is plenty of heat to go around. Roberto told me that he and his friends would try to find Señors Mullet and Jeff, but not to expect much.

"By the way, amigo, just how valuable is the gold disc that you have? I mean, could a guy hock it or something?"

"No, Hector," I said with a laugh. "It's definitely not your everyday pawn-shop item."

The phone rang as Hector was leaving, and Katie laughed when he and I both flinched. The call was from Dave Bentley, at Com-Tech.

"Look, Stick," he said. His voice betrayed his nervous state. "I did some snooping around. I can't prove anything, but it all makes sense. There's a gal here named Martha Denton. She used to be Com-Tech's star computerhead—until Jim Woods came along and pushed her into the background. I should have thought of Denton before. Everybody dislikes her, always have, but the word is that she blames Jim for that too. Everybody's heard her putting him down at one time or another.

"She's a sullen little woman at best—doesn't relate well with others at all—and it turns out that she's the one who claims to have seen Jimmy mucking around where he shouldn't have been, copying data off the operating system or some such."

"We'll need to talk to her," I said. "What's her extension?"

"Three thirty-four," Dave said. "I wouldn't tell her who you are if I were you. Any friend of Jim Woods, you know?"

I thanked him and hung up. Nothing like a bitter fellow

employee to stir up shades of nasty deeds.

"She makes as much as Jim did," Katie said, "but she drives a Yugo with no air. Jimmy once told me that everybody calls it Martha's Broom."

"I see."

"No, you don't see," Katie said seriously. "This lady hated Jim. I should have thought of her right off."

"So, suppose you're right?" I said. "What if Martha did hate Jim enough to kill him, where does the disc fit in? And what about Mullet and Jeff?"

Katie shrugged. "I don't know. But it's after nine, by the way, and they haven't called."

During our drive-thru breakfast at Burger Man they did call. It could have been Mullet or it could have been Jeff, but whoever it was, he claimed to have Jerry Wagner, and made it clear that they wanted the laser storage disc in exchange for his life.

"I want to talk to Jerry," I told him, trying to hide the fear I was feeling. Katie leaned across the console and held her ear up near mine. Fear or no fear, her perfume was intoxicating, and her hair was soft against my face. I heard a muffled "don't try anything" just before Jerry came on the line.

"Stick? Is that you?"

"Yeah, Jerry. Sorry to have gotten you into this. Are you okay? I mean, have they hurt you?"

"No. I guess I'm all right, all things considered. But these guys are serious about that disc. I'm sorry I told them you had it, but I'm no Arnold Schwarzenegger . . . and they know where I live."

"It's okay," I said. "I'd have done exactly the same thing. Do you think they'll honor a trade?"

"I don't know—hummph!—I'm supposed to say yes," Jerry said, catching his breath. "I think they just want the disc."

"All right then, I'll let Meghan know you're all right, and

we'll do the trade as soon as we can. Let me talk to the guy with his arm in a sling."

"What? Neither of these guys has a bad arm—"

Somebody grabbed away the phone, told me where and when to bring the disc, and hung up.

12

I HADN'T PARTICULARLY LIKED the game from the beginning, but if I'd had half a clue who was playing, things might have been a little easier to handle. As it was, I felt real confused. If Mullet and Jeff didn't kidnap Jerry, then who did? White hats? That seemed highly improbable. Why would the white hats use a stolen car? Had Mullet, Jeff, and/or the white hats all gone home and forgotten the whole thing? That wishful thought was a sad joke. And who killed Jim Woods? Katie and I had stepped into the proverbial hornet's nest, and there were more hornets arriving home by the minute.

Katie was more surprised than I was. "If they're not Mullet and Jeff," she asked, "then who are they?"

I shrugged. It seemed odd to me that, for the moment, Katie appeared more interested in who we were meeting than in how dangerous it would be.

"I'm going in to use the sandbox," she said, crumpling up the wrapper from her breakfast muffin and finishing her coffee, "and call home. My folks will be worrying. Here, give me your trash."

Katie opened the door, got out, and proceeded to police the entire inside of my car. Seeing all the aromatic fast-food memorabilia in her arms at one time was a little embarrassing. Worse than that, I wasn't through playing with the old Jolly Meal box she was carrying toward the fat Burger Man–shaped trash receptacle.

I squinted in through the tinted glass picture window and watched Katie conduct a brief but animated conversation at the public pay phone near the rest rooms inside. When she returned, it was clear that her logical, well-organized mind had been busy, even in the "sandbox."

"Look," she said, "we've got to go back to your house, right? How many ways are there into Melbourne . . . three, maybe four? Never mind," she cut me off, "we need a different car—a rental, or maybe Joe Stetler's so you can drive. Do they rent cars with hand controls?"

"Yes," I said. "The three biggest companies do—"

"Anyway," she continued, uninterested in my answer, "if we're going to get back to your house, and if we're going to get the disc, and if we're going to get away—out to the trade site by ten o'clock—we're going to have to get a new look. Everybody knows this car by now."

I had been about to tell Katie Newman that I wasn't going to take her back to Melbourne, let alone to the exchange, but, somehow, this didn't seem like the right time. Besides, her thinking was right on. Formidable, in fact.

"Isn't there a Wheels' game late this afternoon?" she went on. "We'll see Stet there. And you were going to call Meghan Wagner?"

Yes, ma'am.

"Yes," I assured Meghan, only moments later, "Jerry is fine. If we bring the . . . ah, item they want, and if we aren't followed—do you understand that part, Mrs. Wagner?—then I think they really will give Jerry to us. We're going to do exactly what they ask."

Almost, I thought. I promised to call her later that night, or better yet, bring Jerry home. Once again, I don't think I sounded as confident as I would have liked. Now, all I had to do was get myself through the rest of the day mentally. Ten o'clock seemed like a lifetime away. For Jerry, it probably seemed longer than that.

Katie had never seen the puppies run, so, after I called Todd, got him started on the next column, and instructed him to interview Martha Denton, the "broom rider" at Com-Tech, I suggested we pass the time at the dog track next to Hector's place.

The afternoon very nearly got off to a bad start. I left Katie reading her program and forced my way to the nearby bank machine. It's still tough getting blood from a turnip or water from a rock, but getting cash from a plastic charge card is far too easy. I set the five twenties on my lap for only a second while I slipped the credit card back in my wallet, but that was enough.

"Hey!" I shouted at the greasy kid in black Converse high tops and a dirty blue denim jacket, but he scooped the bills off my lap and disappeared into the crowd before I could do anything else. I was about to shout for security, when I heard a loud yelp, followed almost immediately by a murmuring disturbance in the crowd ahead.

A blue-blazered track security officer appeared from nowhere and moved the crowd quickly back out of the way. There, only a dozen yards from the scene of the crime, my cash snatcher lay on the floor, moaning in agony.

"I think he tripped," Katie said to the track official as I rolled up. My money was nowhere to be seen. I started to bring that important matter up, but Katie's unmistakable glance cut the words off in my throat.

"Poor guy went right down in front of me and landed against this concrete pillar. You'd better get him an ambulance. I wonder if he has a good lawyer?"

"My arm," the boy muttered, looking sidelong at Katie

with great distaste. He held the limb close against his side
but said no more. With the unspoken word *lawsuit* flashing
almost visibly over his head, the well-dressed security man
wasted no time gently-but-firmly ushering the injured boy
away.

I almost spoke up again, but Katie shoved five crumpled
twenty-dollar bills discreetly into my hand and winked
knowingly. "We are still hiding out," she said softly, "aren't
we?"

"Well, yes, but—"

"Never mind about *but*. Just show me how we bet that
wad."

Yes, ma'am.

The matinee greyhound races turned out to be a string of
upsets and my famous "dart board" betting technique and
Katie's "first impression" approach worked out pretty well.
She had a ball, like a child enjoying her first day of summer
vacation after a long and grueling school year. After winning
$14.20 on the first race, she really got into it. She picked
dogs by their color, by her favorite numbers (she likes seven),
and by various schoolyard selection chants. I watched her
rush back and forth from the rail to the ticket window in a
whirlwind of excitement. Every time the race caller drawled
out his famous "Heeerrre commmmes the bunny!" Katie
laughed again and shouted encouragement to her canine
picks as they burst from the starting box, sped past her, and
chased the metal silhouette rabbit for all they were worth.
Maybe it was nervous tension, and maybe this was a good
place to let it out, but whatever, I wished the day would never
end.

But it did end. After the eighth race—there are twelve altogether—I had to pry the racing form from Katie's sweaty
hand and usher her to the car. All-in-all, we did quite well.
Counting parking, admission, refreshments, and bets, we

were only twenty-six dollars poorer. Considering that we bet and rebet our money on each of eight races, I told Katie it was a good afternoon. Somehow, I was sure that any afternoon with Katie Newman would be a good one. Tonight would likely be another story.

The Orlando Orange Wheels beat Tampa by three points. Sam scored five buckets from the floor, one of those a three-pointer, and four of five free throws for a total of fifteen points. Joe Stetler had twenty-three, and Eddie Stiggins had nineteen. I sat out. Watching Sam distract her opponents with friendly, seemingly innocent, chitchat, only to leave them in the dust just in time to work a picture perfect give-and-go with Stet is just as enjoyable as watching Magic Johnson and Michael Jordan—maybe more. Still, it's hard to enjoy anything when your guts are steadily working themselves into knots.

Stet gave over his keys, pleading with me not to get the "classic" Monte shot up. Then Sam planted a lip lock on me that nearly popped the dimes out of my penny loafers.

"Don't you get shot up," she said firmly. "I'm not nearly through with you. Anyway, you owe me dinner."

I thought her sideways glance at Katie Newman was unusually cool, but wasn't about to say so.

Katie and I took Route 192 to Interstate 95, drove down to the Malabar/Palm Bay exit, and approached Melbourne on Highway 1 from the south. The black '86 Monte Carlo SS not only looks better than my Z28 Camaro, it has more guts too. Its fuel-injected, 350-cubic-inch engine is tuned to perfection, but then my Camaro has a few more miles—72,307 more to be exact.

"Here," Katie said, fitting me with a pair of dark, wrap-around sunglasses. "They'll be looking for people who look like us, so let's look like somebody else."

She dug around in her flight bag and came out with a white corduroy baseball cap and readjusted the leather back strap so it fit my head.

"There! I'd hardly recognize you myself!" she said.

I glanced at myself in the rearview mirror and found that the *Terminator* look gained with the shades was lost quickly when balanced with the goofy Jayhawk on the hat. Someday I would have to get even with that bird.

Katie retrieved her bandanna, tied it loosely around her neck, and tucked her red hair up under a heavily autographed painter's cap. The only name I could read without driving off the road was Scooter Barry, so I assumed that the wrinkled hat had been signed by the remaining NCAA Basketball Champions as well. At least there was no sign of their mascot.

Palm Bay and Melbourne run together in a string of communities, so "the edge of town" is really no more than a sun-faded sign. But a sign can take on pronounced significance when you are experiencing a high level of paranoia. Even with the air-conditioning running at max, I perspired profusely. The area between Stet's 9mm and my ribs was a swampland. Whenever the car bounced and the holster swung briefly away from my body, I could feel rivulets of sweat run all the way to my hip.

"Slow down a little, Stick. We don't want to get stopped for speeding."

Katie's warning interrupted the rising panic inside me and returned most of my attention to the task at hand. After some heated discussion en route, I reluctantly agreed to let Katie run in the back door of my house and grab the disc while I pulled around the block, picking her up when she came out the front. She had not hesitated to remind me that she was considerably faster in every aspect of the assignment, but the whole thing didn't sit well.

Oh, I knew she was right; Katie could probably have

beaten me before I was paralyzed. And whereas I would have had to unload the wheelchair, go in and out the front door, and load the chair back in the car when I was through, she would not be so limited. When she explained her plan, it was both logical and formidable. But this wasn't just a race.

Somebody—maybe several somebodies—would surely be watching my house. Good guys, bad guys, who knows? They might not recognize me in Stet's car, and I might even let Katie out at the Crenshaws' without drawing any undue attention, but when she walked through their carport, hopped their back fence, and sprinted across my backyard and through my laundry room door, things might get hairy real fast.

Don and Betty Crenshaw's twin Ford Escorts were gone. Don bowls on Saturday nights and Betty plays bridge at her sister's. I pulled into their drive, under the carport, and shut off the engine and the lights. Everything looked normal in the neighborhood, but that didn't fool me for a minute. Stet's leather steering wheel cover was soaked with my sweat, and my heart pounded so hard I thought it was trying to get out of my chest.

Dear Lord, I thought prayerfully, I'm a writer. I don't know what I'm doing here and I sure could use some help.

"Stick?"

"Mm?"

"You okay?"

"Of course not! You got the gun?"

Katie pulled up the left leg of her red KU sweatpants. The derringer was taped to the inside of her leg, just above the ankle.

"Where'd you learn that little trick?"

"Don Johnson," she said with a grin. "*Miami Vice!*"

Good grief.

"Well, shall we do this deal or what?" she said, looking at me expectantly.

"Do I have a choice?"

"No."

"Okay," I said, not feeling that there was anything okay about it. "See you on the other side."

"Aren't you forgetting something, Stick?"

"Huh?"

"The disc. You never told me where you put the laser disc."

Suddenly I knew one reason why the whole thing didn't sit well. Something deep in my gut resisted the idea of turning the disc over to anyone, at least without getting Jerry back first. But that was stupid. This was Katie Newman.

$\triangledown$

1 3

THE FRECKLES ON KATIE'S nose reacted much as they had to the Preparation H, but she leaned over, kissed my cheek, and tousled the hair on the back of my neck.

"Sam's right," she said. "You really are something, Stick Foster."

She was over the fence before I pulled myself together, cranked up the Monte, and started around the block. For the atheist, there is the foxhole conversion, and for those who believe in a Creator, there is the irresistible urge to negotiate: "God, if you'll only get me through this one, I'll . . ." Unfortunately, I just couldn't think of anything valuable enough to offer.

I turned west at the south end of the block, then north up my street. There were no obviously out-of-place cars in sight, but that didn't release any of the knots in my shoulders or my stomach. I stared at my front door as I moved farther up the block. Katie should already be coming across the lawn to meet me. By the time I reached my driveway, I was nearly at a full stop. My heart had found a new potential escape route, it was trying to hack its way out through my eardrums. Where was she?

Somebody's screen door slammed nearby as I pulled to a complete stop at the curb in front of my house. It wasn't until I heard screeching tires, out of sight around the north end of the block, that I realized I had just heard my own screen door slam. Somebody had exited my back door in a hurry.

I floored the Monte and left smoking rubber all the way to the corner. Oblivious to who or what might be coming the other way, I cranked wide around the turn and raced east, looking for disappearing taillights. There were none.

Back at the house, I fumbled frantically with the front door key. Stet's 9mm lay on my lap. If there was a way to hold the weapon at the ready and push my wheelchair through the door, I didn't know what it was. Reaching in quickly, I flipped on the bank of light switches (just inside on the living room wall) and leaned back out of the way. Lights came on in the living room, the hallway, and on the front porch, but nothing else happened.

I shoved into the room, picking up the automatic as I rolled across the threshold, and looked first into the kitchen, then down the hallway. Nothing.

"Katie!" I yelled, not caring who might be listening. Let them come. "Katie, are you all right!"

Fear, anger, and physical disability make for a most unpleasant combination. I eased down the hallway and turned slowly into my bedroom. The shadowed movement came from my left, but I had no time to train the handgun on it. Throwing up my left arm just in time to ward off the attack, my elbow caught Butkis midleap and sent him sprawling back against the waterbed with a screech. The poor guy's tail was puffed out to three times its normal size. For a second, I thought my heart had really escaped. Instead, it had just stopped all together.

When it started beating again, and when I was able to get my breath, I searched the house, room by room, each room twice. Katie Newman was gone. The thought of trading the

disc for either Jerry Wagner or Katie Newman was a nightmare of despair. As I rolled back toward the laundry room, I
knew that I didn't have any choice. Jerry and his captors
would be expecting me in less than thirty minutes.

I hadn't noticed while looking for Katie, but much of
Butkis's litter was spilled over the edges of the plastic tray.
Still, I sifted through much of what remained before it struck
me that not only was Katie Newman missing, but the laser
disc as well.

After reporting the abduction to Rita Daley, dispatcher at
the MPD—and assuring her that no, I couldn't come in to
see the chief just then—I called Phil and, in case his line was
bugged, gave him some cryptic instructions about meeting
me. Moments later, I watched him pull into Wanda's drive-
in, leave his pickup, and walk into the "home of the Wanda
Burger." When nobody followed him, I pulled around back
and met him in the alley by the kitchen door. Wrapped up
in his windbreaker, Phil carried a sawed-off Ithaca model 37,
12-gauge pump shotgun.

"Who we gonna shoot?" he asked, putting the old gun on
the floor.

"I don't know."

I told him about the fine mess I was in and asked if he
had any suggestions.

"Besides going home?"

"Yeah," I said, "besides that."

There wasn't much time for an elaborate plan, but Phil
ended up in the trunk with his shotgun and the car phone.
He cut off the phone's cigarette lighter power plug, spliced
the unit directly into one of Stet's taillight wires, and then
jerry-rigged the trunk latch so he could get out by himself.

I followed the directions I had been given that morning and
turned east off Highway 1 at Oak Hill. After two turns on

two dirt roads, I could smell the saltwater aroma of Mosquito Lagoon, that section of the Intercoastal Waterway that runs from Titusville to South Daytona. Unlike the more familiar waterfront areas near Melbourne, things around Oak Hill were largely deserted. I tried to avoid scratching up the Monte's side panels on the passing palmetto fronds, but wasn't doing very well. I'd heard that the shrimping was supposed to be good out here in the "northern" boonies, but I'd never come myself. Until now. Now, I wanted to go home.

The light afternoon coastal showers had left brown puddles in the jeep trail's low spots. They showed up well enough in the headlights, but the depth of each was impossible to guess. After bottoming out several times and grimacing under the accompanying barrage of protestations from the trunk, I learned to slow way down. Then I worried about getting stuck. Contorted palm trees and scrub oak draped in Spanish Moss passed like specters in the muggy Florida night, and the dense palmettos on either side walled me in as effectively as barbed wire fence. There was no turning back.

When the sandy trail suddenly opened into a wide clearing on the banks of Mosquito Lagoon, the growing claustrophobia gave way to a feeling of being overexposed. As if to deliberately justify my fears, a set of powerful high beams blazed on, accompanied by another spotlight, up and to the right. All the blinding white light was focused on my sweaty face. I stopped the car.

"This is it, Phil," I whispered, wondering whether he could hear me, afraid to speak louder.

A bullhorn-enhanced voice cut through the night. "Turn off the lights and the engine. Then get out. Slowly."

I did what I was told. Wheelchairs and sand never have been particularly compatible, but there was nowhere to run in any case. Under my half-zipped windbreaker, Stet's 9mm felt as if it weighed fifty pounds. I suddenly wished that I had left it in the car. What if they, whoever "they" were, saw it? In all the light, how could they help but see the monstrous, throbbing bulge in my left armpit? Even if they didn't see it right away, what good did it do me? They could have been all around me for all I knew.

I sat behind the open driver's door with my hands in the air, fighting the almost irresistible urge to stare into the blinding lights like a rabbit on the highway. An understanding of the absolute and total stupidity of what I was doing came to me fully in that moment, but the insight was scarce help in my time of need.

"You have something for us, I believe."

The bullhorn was gone, but the quiet voice, somewhere out in the humid darkness, had more than enough authority in and of itself. When God spoke to Moses, out of the burning bush, I suspect He used just that tone.

"I want to see Jerry first." I sounded like a whining youngster, my voice too high, breaking at the edges.

A car door opened and someone, a tall black silhouette, was shoved roughly in front of the blinding headlights.

"Jerry?" My voice wasn't getting any better. I tried shielding my eyes, but it was no good. "Is that you?"

"Yeah, Stick," he said. "I'm here."

"You okay?"

"As well as you I suppose, right about now."

"I know what you mean. Look, we've got a little problem."

"You don't say."

"I mean another problem."

"Great."

"What problem?" the voice of god interrupted. Jerry was jerked back into the darkness and the car door was slammed with unmistakable finality.

"Well," I said, "it's about the laser disc."

"Yes?" The almighty was displeased.

"It wouldn't do you any good to hurt Jerry or me. The disc is gone."

"Gone!" That was pure swallowed-up-by-the-earth wrath there.

"Yes. Someone stole the disc from my house and kidnapped the girl. There was nothing I could do."

After what seemed like long seconds of silence, punctuated by an acrid smell that seemed out of place in the salty lagoon, god said, "You'll have to come with us." But my fear disappeared in the ensuing chaos.

"Where is Wagner?" shouted the voice of god. The car door opened and closed, harder than before.

"I don't know!" hissed a nearby archangel. "He was here a second ago."

"What's burning?"

"No!"

The headlights on the kidnappers' car went out first, as a burst of colored fire erupted just inside the windshield; then the spotlight flashed briefly and died.

"Get Foster!" god commanded. But I was already waving a 9mm wildly in the direction of the sparkling electrical fire and turning on the Monte's headlights. Phil's Model 37 punctuated the turn of the proverbial tables and from somewhere in the nearby jungle he told them to throw their weapons to me and lie facedown in the sand. Phil's voice was not quite the same as god's, but it had the same general effect.

Two things struck me as the dashboard fire grew out of control inside the steel-gray Chrysler sedan. First, the white hats (who else would be standing next to a mosquito-infested swamp, in the middle of the night, in three-piece suits?) weren't armed. That is, they had guns, but in response to Phil's order, they both reached into their coats to retrieve weapons that I had assumed were already trained on Jerry and me. Second, despite their governmental rank and world-renowned training, both men (even the taller one with a facial bruise, presumably from his recent fender bender with the Melbourne police) seemed quite small and nonthreatening as they lay cursing in the sand. And Meghan Wagner was right—the little guy was little.

I aimed Stet's automatic nervously, first at one of them, then at the other. But it felt like a rather pointless exercise.

▽

14

"THEY'VE GOT GUNS on their ankles too," Jerry said, coming up behind me. "And who knows where else, but I don't think they're authorized to hurt us."

"Lose them anyway!" Phil shouted at the white hats as he pushed out of the palmettos to my left. "Throw 'em away real careful."

"Look," the fallen deity said, tossing a second automatic pistol out onto the sand, "that disc may be of major importance to national security. We had to find you and secure it."

"I'm sure Mrs. Wagner will understand," I said, my voice returning, complete with my witty flare for sarcasm.

"Mrs. Wagner has already been told. She was willingly helping us catch you."

Ouch.

Phil insisted that our conversation be brief, assuring the disgruntled FBI agents that the Volusia County sheriff's department, or perhaps the nearest Division of Forestry Ranger, would eventually spot the flames that had engulfed the Chrysler's seat covers and now climbed out the windows and stretched into the night sky. Added to the already crumpled front end, the poor car was just not having a good week.

Our disgruntled friends tried hard to talk some sense into us before we took our leave of them. Agent god put forth several scenarios wherein the laser disc and its advanced parallel processing technology was bound for unfriendly hands. Katie Newman played prominently in all of them. The first of the bureau's two favorite story lines made the befreckled redhead out as a radical antispace groupie working, directly or indirectly, for Senator Benjamin Holcum of Louisiana. Her "engagement" to Jim Woods, they suggested, was a well-executed act of premeditated infiltration.

The second theory wasn't any better. Maybe worse. Katie, they said, might be working for a foreign government, most probably Middle Eastern, whose goal was to steal the programming technique, embarrass the United States, and possibly damage the shuttle program in the process.

"That's all very well," I said, interrupting the zealous agent's distasteful speculation, "but we just can't help you."

"Too bad about that faulty wiring. I'd move away some," Phil added, climbing into the Monte's backseat with my wheelchair. "If they're not here in the next ten minutes or so, that gas tank will go like a twenty-pound claymore mine."

I spun the mud-splattered Chevy around (unintentionally spraying damp sand on my government's tireless servants) and heeded Phil's suggestion to make haste. He told us that he called the Sheriff's Department before slipping out of the trunk and shorting out the feds dashboard wiring. I considered shouting a parting shot about watching out for coral snakes, but thought better of it. After all, despite present appearances, they were supposed to be the good guys. At least they still thought they were.

"I didn't know about Meghan, Stick," Jerry said. "Honest."

"I know that, Jerry. What do you think about their story? Is there anything on that disc that could threaten our national security?"

"That seems pretty farfetched, but the obvious possibility

is bad enough. That software controls the communication between the range safety officers and the shuttle, right? Suppose someone altered the software so that they could bypass the system and give their own destruct command?"

"Dave Bentley says it can't be done," I said, not at all certain that I believed it now. "He says no transmitter in this hemisphere could even come close. He told me the computer equipment at Com-Tech might not be the latest, but those three transmitters are not only state-of-the-art, they are, well, big . . . real big."

"Then I don't know, Stick," Jerry said. "Maybe I need to lean on Trish Taylor. If there's something funny in that program, she can probably find it if she wants to."

"And why are there two files on there, Jerry? How do we know they're identical?"

"Well, we don't know that for sure—the value tables alone would take months to compare visually—but when any two files that size take up the same number of storage bytes, chances are *real* good that one is a backup of the other. You use a word processor, don't you?"

"Sure. Why?"

"Your newspaper column runs, what, about eight hundred words?"

"About that."

"And you've been writing five of them a week for, what, two years?"

"Yeah. So?"

"How many of those five hundred plus or minus columns take up the same number of storage bytes in your computer's directory listing?"

"Ah. I see what you mean," I said as the idea settled in. "Even with a three- or four-page manuscript, I can't remember seeing any two exactly alike."

"So you see what I mean about two programs with enough code to fill a stack of phone books."

Mm.

"What about the girl, Stick?" Phil said softly, after a couple of moments of silence. "What do you think?"

I'd been deliberately trying to push that part of the
"unofficial" conversation out of my mind, but Phil was right,
I couldn't pretend. And the FBI didn't have her—didn't know
where she was. At least that's what Agent god told us. So
who did? To my mind, the most likely answer led back to
Phil's friends, Mullet and Jeff. Unfortunately, the same two
theories so popular with the bureau also worked for these
two, as yet, unidentified men. That wasn't good. Katie could
be either their competitor . . . or their accomplice.

One way or the other, Agent god had insisted, Jim Woods,
like Samson, strong man of Old Testament Israel, had to have
been cooperating on some level. If that was true, it was too bad
he couldn't have taken the bad guys with him when he died.

"I don't know, Phil," I said, my throat tightening around
the words. "It all makes some sense, but my heart says 'no
way.' Anyhow, I've got to find her. I have to see for myself."

"We've been a pretty good team from the start," Phil said,
reaching up and putting his big hand on my shoulder. "How
about letting me tag along?"

"Thanks, Phil. I was hoping you'd say that. Being gimped-
up's not quite so bad when you've got the real Rambo on
your side!"

"Even when I found out I wasn't in any real danger, I know
I was glad to see him," Jerry said with a laugh. "Thanks.
Both of you."

Yo!

Joe Stetler wasn't at all happy. Not about being awakened at
2 A.M., not about the scratches and the mud along both sides
of his "classic" black Monte Carlo SS. While Phil rerigged the
cellular phone and installed it back in my Camaro, Jerry and
I tried to explain the night's adventure to the disgruntled

double amputee. When we drove away, he was still rolling his wheelchair around the dinged-up Chevy, reciting a litany of colorful words undoubtedly left over from his brief military career.

On the way to Sam's apartment, I called Todd Gulick. He wasn't real excited about my timing either, but once fully awake, proved to be a wealth of information. Not all of it was good. The Martha Denton story was much as Dave Bentley had told us. No one liked her, and she made no bones about disliking Jim Woods. That he should die, "selling out his country," as she put it, was, in her eyes, most fitting. According to Ms. Martha, Jim was never that good anyway.

"She's a pretty classic paranoid, Stick," Todd said. "You know, 'nobody really appreciates me, everybody's jealous and out to get me.' And she seldom passed up an opportunity to put Woods down. Several co-workers even heard her brag about how easy it would be to trash Jim's program. But her actual employment record is flawless."

We both agreed that she was worth watching, so I told Todd to go ahead and hire a free-lancer to follow her around for a few days. I'd talk Randy into paying for it later.

Then came the bad news. Todd had done some background checking on Katie Newman. Maybe "tried" is more accurate.

"According to the enrollment officer, Katie Newman entered the University of Kansas grad school last fall," he told me, "the same semester that Senator Holcum's big debate was held there. Before that, her transcript says she attended a Geneva College and a Jefferson Community College. I found a Jefferson Parish Community College . . . as in New Orleans . . . as in Senator Holcum's home turf. I'm trying to track that down and go back from there, but it just sort of dead-ends."

"What about Holcum?" I asked the sleepy junior reporter. "Is he so determined to scrap the space program that he'd be involved with all this?"

"I've got copies of several Ben Holcum speeches, Stick.

He's fire and brimstone against the whole industry—says it's taking food out of the mouths of the hungry and all that—and he doesn't mind raising the *Challenger* specter to help soften folks up to his point of view, but I don't know about kidnapping and murder. Some of his more radical disciples, though . . . who knows?"

"Well, keep on it," I told him. "If you find out anything more on Katie Newman, I want to know."

I called from the parking lot, and Sam Wagner came to the door of her apartment, wearing a yellow nightshirt with a chorus line of teddy bears across the front. Her golden hair was tousled and her eyes were puffed with sleep. Sam's everyday chair was little more than a seat on wheels. The backrest had been cut down nearly to nothing and the footrests were gone. A gray seat-belt-like strap stretched across the lower frame, near the tiny, solid front casters, and Sam's feet rested on the strap, her toes barely clearing the floor.

While I stared, Jerry walked in and gave his sister a hug. Phil slapped me on the back and we followed them into the living room. Jerry introduced Phil Stilles and told Sam about the rescue and the semiphony kidnapping. I told her about Katie.

"I was wondering, Sam," I said, "whether you'd run Jerry home and maybe let Phil and me spend the night. We'll be out of your hair in the morning."

"You have a standing invitation, Stick." She was smiling and I was blushing. "If you choose to bring your friends along," she winked at Phil, "what can I say? Hold on a minute, Jer. I'll throw something on and get my keys."

Jerry phoned his wife, chiding her gently for her performance, and then left with Sam. I collapsed on the sofa. Phil went back out to retrieve the car phone, turned on the mute switch, then commandeered the recliner by the window.

"What next?" he asked.

"Sleep. Then, I don't have a clue."

▽

15

I DREAMED THAT SAM Wagner's body was close against me,
her lips lightly brushing mine. But instead of her perfume,
I smelled the unmistakable aroma of black coffee. When I
opened my eyes, she handed me the steaming mug.

Sam sat parked against the edge of the sofa, her mischie-
vous grin warm and sunny above me. Phil was snoring lightly
in the big chair by the window, and each of us had been covered with a light blanket.

"Come on, sleepy," she said, pointing to the blinking red
light on my portable phone. "You're developing quite a back-
log here, and if we're going to find your Ms. Newman, we'd
better get on it."

"What do you mean, 'we,'" I said, flipping off the mute
switch and dialing the service. "You're not getting on anything."

Samantha raised an eyebrow, grinned at me, and took a
second cup of coffee over to where Phil now sat yawning and
rubbing his eyes. While I wrote down the various names and
numbers of people who had called the service while I slept,
they appeared to be discussing me, but I couldn't make any
of it out. Two of the calls had priority: Todd Gulick and the

Fonze. Whether Officer Sanchez was still upset with me or
not, I needed his help. And he deserved an explanation. It
went better than I thought.

"You okay?"

"Yeah, Fonze. Thanks."

"I've never seen anything like it, Stick. There are feds from
agencies I never heard of swarming all over the coast. You
were in some real deep refuse, but they say you don't have
what they're looking for anymore. Is that true?"

"And you also know that I lost Katie Newman, Fonze. Any
word?"

"Nothing."

"I'm going to need all the help I can get if I'm going to find
her before they do. Or before something happens to her."

"They say she's bad news, Stick."

"Mm."

In the end, he agreed to do what he could—without in-
curring the wrath of the various white hats with whom all
department personnel were ordered to cooperate.

Todd filled me in on the next shuttle's news.

"The 'official' line is 'technical difficulties,' Stick—something about engine tests—but all of our sources on the inside
say that's a crock. Everybody's whispering sabotage, but nobody knows anything about how. They're dissecting Jim
Woods's software every which way, testing it ten times a day,
but not coming up with anything—at least as far as Dave
Bentley can tell. He's gotten kind of cool lately, Stick. You
don't suppose he's in this somehow, do you?"

"Nothing would surprise me at this point. Keep an eye on
him. Maybe he's got good reason to be afraid of too much
scrutiny."

"Anyway," Todd went on, "the president is apparently putting big pressure on NASA to get the *Discovery* up on schedule.
That means no delays if they can help it. And the security is
so tight, you couldn't get a trained chameleon in there.

"By all accounts, Martha Denton is back in the number-one spot at Com-Tech, and the gal I've got following her says she goes home, reads *U.S. News & World Report*, and goes to bed. No visitors. No phone calls. Nothing.

"Randy wants your head, by the way. You'd better call him."

"But aren't we getting him some great press for his press?" I said.

"Oh, he loves that part. It's the part about the renegade reporter out of his control that irritates him."

"Tell him to take the 'I'm behind my reporter all the way' approach and kick everybody out of his office."

"You tell him."

I told Todd I'd think about it, asked him to stop and feed Butkis, and urged him to pull out all the stops in an effort to find Mullet and Jeff. "If they're still around, somebody's seen them."

He promised to stay on it. I finished my coffee, climbed into my chair, and headed for the bathroom.

"Where to first?" Phil asked.

"I don't know about you two," I said without looking back, "but I'm going to church."

It didn't surprise me when Sam and Phil both passed on attending the small Presbyterian church in downtown Orlando, so I told them I'd be back in a couple of hours. In the midst of chaos, the thought of going to church had its own merits, but I had other motives as well.

I took Robinson Avenue east into downtown and turned north at Lake Eola Park. Bright blue water, emanating from the dome-shaped island fountain, danced in the Sunday morning sun while ducks and elderly joggers waddled around the shoreline. The old white stucco church sits on a corner, a block from the lake, and neatly dressed parishioners filed up the tall front steps.

Fortunately, I discovered a wheelchair ramp on the building's west side, where the black asphalt parking lot was nearly full. I found a spot in the back corner of the lot, against the chain-link fence, where no one would be able to park too close and block my door. Two young girls in almost matching pastel dresses hurried up the ramp ahead of me and held open the door at the top. I greeted and thanked them on my way in, so didn't notice, until it was too late, that I had entered a side door at the front, not the rear, of the small sanctuary.

Two hundred pairs of friendly but curious eyes were fixed firmly upon me, and turning hastily around in the aisle and parking next to the front pew didn't relieve the weight of them. It only shifted their focus to the back of my head, where I suddenly felt an irresistible urge to scratch. Fortunately, the preacher chose that moment to appear through a door in the wood-paneled front wall of the sanctuary and mount the three steps to the pulpit.

Now, far from grave-side responsibilities, his smile attracted me at once. As he greeted his flock, welcomed the visitors, and read the week's announcements, I knew immediately that this man was a shepherd. Before he died, my father used to rag about all the "phony, con-man preachers" who passed themselves off as shepherds of God's flock. "Show biz," he'd say. "They're turning the church into high-dollar show biz. A real minister is a servant, a shepherd who cares more for his sheep than he does for himself. Find a real shepherd," Dad told me often, "and you'll find a real church." Dad wouldn't be happy if he knew how long it had been since I'd attended any church on a regular basis.

The bulletin in the pew rack said the pastor's name was Robert McClarrin, and it wasn't until he announced the opening musical selection that I realized two things: first, there was no organ; and second, there were no hymnals. The reddish brown tome in the pew was called *The Book of Psalms for Singing*, and, indeed, it included various letter-coded selections of all 150 biblical songs of praise and supplication. The congregation, including a modest choir, was skillfully directed by a short man in a dark blue suit and black glasses. When we sang Psalm 45, selection A, the a cappella harmony went right to the depths of my soul.

> My heart doth overflow;
> A noble theme I sing.
> My tongue's a skillful writer's pen
> To speak about the King.

The sermon was from Matthew, chapter five, and Bob Mc-Clarrin reminded his flock lovingly that we could murder each other with our words, just as surely as with knives of steel. My Dad would have been pleased.

When the congregation dispersed, I met with the pastor in his study. He would not tolerate "Reverend," and insisted that I call him Bob.

"I remember seeing you at the cemetery," he said, "and, of course, the *Sentinel* picks up your column with some regularity."

I smiled, feeling drawn to the congenial man, but somewhat disadvantaged since I didn't know anything about him.

"Gene and Edna have spoken of you as well," Pastor Bob went on. "They've been wondering about Katie—we all have. Is she well?"

"That's why I came," I said. "She's gone. And whether or not she is in danger depends on who she is. I was hoping you could tell me something about that."

Bob McClarrin shook his head, and his eyes told me that I'd made little sense. He shook his head often as I explained the official line on Katie Newman. "I thought maybe you could tell me more about her," I concluded, "or at least about Jim—something to help me make up my own mind."

"I counsel every couple who ask me to perform a wedding for them," Bob said with a firmness that defied his kindly nature. "Especially when one of them is a member of this church, leader of the young people's group, and a son of dear friends. Jim met me once a week, over lunch or in the evening, for months. Whenever Katie was here, they came together."

"Jim Woods would be the last person on earth I'd ever suspect of anything like that," Pastor Bob went on. "First, the money would mean little to him. He lived in the small house his grandfather left the family. He hardly knew what to do with the money he made as it was. He spent a lot of it on the kids here at church.

"Second, even though he never dated much—in fact, Katie was his first real love interest—he didn't have the usual headlong rush syndrome so typical of young men in their first affair of the heart. I think Katie would have married him several months after they met at a church conference on Lookout Mountain, near Chattanooga, Tennessee. No, Jimmy wanted to do it once, the right way. Like many brilliant folks, he had a compulsion to think and rethink every new situation, comparing and analyzing all the possible courses of action. That's what made him so good with computers."

"And did he have doubts about Katie?"

"Oh, no!" Pastor Bob said with a laugh. "Jim only had doubts about Jim. Outside of his job, he saw his thoroughness as indecisiveness, especially when compared to someone like Katie Newman, who makes decisions on the run as if she were incapable of error. Between the lines of our conversations, I heard him wondering how it was that Katie could be in love with him. No matter how many times he added up the figures, he just couldn't make it compute."

"And Katie?" I said.

"Katie told me that her parents died when she was twelve. She's always had to make decisions for herself. Katie's a liberated lady, but I believe she loved Jim and wanted to marry him for that reason alone. Does that answer your question?"

"It helps," I said, extending my hand. "Thanks."

"Come back," he said, meaning it. "We hate to see that big ramp go to waste!"

$\triangledown$

16

Sᴀᴍ'ѕ ʀᴇᴅ ᴄᴏɴᴠᴇʀᴛɪʙʟᴇ Mᴜѕᴛᴀɴɢ screeched into the church lot as I rolled down the concrete ramp on my rear wheels.

"Hurry up, Stick!" Phil shouted, jumping out of Sam's passenger door. He ran to my Camaro, carrying the car phone and my bundled-up white jacket, with his shotgun poking out of one end and part of Stet's holster hanging out the other. Before I reached the sidewalk, Sam squealed the Mustang's tires on her way back out onto the street. Before I could wave, she was gone.

"No more time for religion, Stick," Phil yelled at me across the parking lot. "Unlock this heap!"

As soon as I opened the door, Phil threw the arsenal on the floor of the car and started hooking up the phone.

"Get in," he said. "They're going to call any second."

"Who's going to call? What's going on?"

"Maybe Mullet and Jeff, I don't know," Phil said as I pulled my wheelchair in behind the driver's seat and fastened my safety belt. "Somebody phoned the paper and talked to Todd. He gave them this number. They want to trade Katie for the disc."

"What? But she . . . they have the disc."

"Apparently not, Sherlock, " Phil said, finishing the phone hookup. "Anyway, if you want Katie, you give them a disc."

"What disc, Phil? We don't have one. These guys don't wear three-piece suits, and they don't need anybody's authorization to blow us away."

"Well, we thought about that, Sam and I—by the way, you were right about her. She's gonna be one heck of a lawyer! Anyway, she's off to her brother, Jerry's, and they're off to Trish what's-her-name's, and then they're off to Morton Manufacturing to 'borrow' a blank disc. Jerry says these thugs probably have no way of knowing whether there's anything on it anyway. We're betting that they're just errand boys for somebody else. Not bad, aye?"

"No, maybe not, Phil, but where's the real disc?"

"That's not my department, Stick. It's your litter box. Personally, I liked the Preparation H better."

"Thanks," I said. "This better work, though. I can't take much more cloak and dagger. And I miss my waterbed."

"Poor boy!"

The phone call, when it came, was not much like the one when Jerry was on the trading block. The caller's command of the English language strained my creationist beliefs, suggesting that he existed on a considerably lower rung of the so-called evolutionary ladder than the white hats. That realization wasn't comforting at all. When I asked to speak with Katie, he told me to engage in various physically paradoxical sexual acts with myself, described a phone booth where I was to bring the disc—alone—and hung up.

"Well?" Phil said as I pulled into the back lot of the Steak & Shake on Highway 50 where we were to wait for Sam. "What do you think?"

"About Katie, or about getting killed?"

"About anything. You're awfully quiet."

"I don't know what to think," I told him.

I'm an aggressive reporter, even if I write mostly fluff. I work hard to produce good human interest stories, but this mess was something else. I sometimes rag at other handicapped individuals for "hiding" behind their disabilities, submitting to unnecessary limitations, failing to get out and mix it up with real life. Right now, real life was a little overwhelming, and the seductive voice of self-pity was whispering something about: why should a crippled reporter stick his neck out for somebody he really doesn't even know?

When Sam whirled into the drive-in lot, followed by Joe Stetler, Eddie Stiggins, and a dozen Orange Wheels, I knew the answer.

"I can't go from phone booth to phone booth with a convoy of gimps!" I said when Stet pulled up alongside.

"You don't have to," Trish Taylor said, getting out of Sam's Mustang and leaning in Phil's window. "Here."

I caught the small box and opened it. The gold disc, I recognized. The tiny silver rectangle in a clear plastic case might have been a computer chip, but meant nothing to me.

"I put two copies of the Woods program on that disc, just in case, but if anything happens to either one of those little trinkets," Trish said emphatically, "my distinguished career at Morton Manufacturing and Aerospace is over."

The diminutive silver gadget—so small that four of them would fit easily on my pinkie fingernail—was a solar-powered microchip transmitter. Trish explained that a friend at Morton had recently designed it and was testing it on bees.

"They want to sell them to the entomologists trying to track the South American killer bees," the gray-haired wizardess said, sticking the tiny devise to the top of my sunroof with a dab of silicone adhesive. "It sends out an infrared signal for an effective range of about one mile. Sam says I should take the receiver and ride with Mr. Stetler." Retrieving what looked like a small radio from the red convertible, she walking around to Stet's scratched-up Monte Carlo. "By the way," she said, pausing to look at me over Stet's roof, "don't park in the shade."

"Sam and Jerry, and the others, will stay back until we need them. We've all got these," Stet said, handing me a portable CB radio. He reached out and dragged a bottle opener casually along my Camaro's rust-ravaged blue door. The squealing sound set my teeth on edge. "There," he said with a grinning sigh, "I feel better now! You ready?"

I would have answered, but everybody was laughing. Nothing really needed to be said anyway. Phil slapped me on the back, handed me Stet's shoulder-rigged 9mm, picked up his shotgun and the CB radio, and got into the trunk. As I pulled out on the highway, I heard a dozen voices behind me singing "Burning Bridges," the Mike Curb tune from *Kelly's Heroes*. We were on our way.

Dear God. Make Katie Newman one of the good guys.

At first, as we headed toward the coast, I could see Stet's black Monte and Sam's red Mustang in my rearview mirror. But by the time we reached Route 95 and headed north, toward the designated phone booth, in Mims, my entourage was nowhere to be seen.

Mims is ten miles north of the cape, a small bedroom community on Route 1 with its own share of touristy paraphernalia. If Jerry hadn't been in the trunk—both times—he would have recognized it as halfway to Oak Hill, the scene of his Mosquito Lagoon rescue-fiasco. The drive-up phone booth was right where it was supposed to be—next to a convenience store on the south end of town—but a fat guy wearing a hat made of beer cans and yarn sat parked in his battered Ford Maverick, chatting merrily and eating cheese puffs.

Ten minutes past the deadline, my car phone rang and the missing link who was tour-directing my trip proceeded to curse me out, demanding to know why the designated phone was busy. I tried to tell him about the fat man, but he was too busy threatening me and elaborating on his extensive familiarity with human anatomy and the sexual practices of certain subspecies, the exact identification of which was never clear to me.

He ignored my request to speak with Katie and sent me to another phone booth. I'm sure the thug brothers had seen all this in a TV movie, and despite the fact that I had a phone, they made me visit most of the public installations inside the city limits. Since more than half of them were out of order or in use, we used my phone most of the time anyway. By the third stop, the profanity sounded like a broken record, but if I were buying the guy a T-shirt, it would say I'M DUMB AS A BROKEN BRICK . . . AND THAT MAKES ME DANGEROUS on the front.

The game finally ended and they sent me to a Lock-Your-Own storage shed complex that was under construction three miles south, between Titusville and La Grange.

The semimammalian voice assured me, replete with colorful adjectives, that my "friend" would die instantly if I tried "anything funny." Following his instructions exactly, and pouring sweat, I drove all the way to the back of the empty construction site, pulled into the last storage unit, and shut off my engine. Then I remembered Trish's admonition about parking in the sun.

I looked up through the sunroof, but the only thing I saw was a dot of white silicone. Either the bee bug was there, or it wasn't. In any case, I had to park somewhere else no matter what Cro-Magnon man had said. Before I could restart the car and back out, Mullet and Jeff were pointing guns in my side windows and grinning viciously.

1 7

Mullet's face looked like a junior high science fair moonscape. His right arm hung in a dirty, makeshift sling, but I had little doubt that he could squeeze the trigger of the .38 in his hand. With the barrel hovering just inches from my left temple, I figured he probably wouldn't miss either. And somehow, the thought that a bullet might find its way into and out of my skull with enough ballistic coefficient left to kill Big Jeff didn't perk me up much.

In the other window, Jeff's nose was a mess. Under any other circumstances, I might have laughed. Now, looking down the barrel of his military Colt .45 automatic, the humor was lost. He reached through the passenger window and yanked Stet's 9mm out from under my windbreaker with a jerk and stuck it in his belt.

"Gonna be a hero, aye?" he said in a painfully nasal tone of voice. "Heroes die in the real world."

"You have something for us?" Mullet said, touching his revolver to my left temple and giving it a shove.

"That depends," I said, trying to breathe in a way that would keep me from passing out. "I want to see Miss Newman."

" 'Miss' Newman is it now? Well aren't we a formal little crip." Mullet smacked the side of my head with his pistol. He gasped involuntarily as the jolt shot back through his damaged arm, but I wasn't in any position to revel in his stupidity. "You listen to me, jerkface! Miss goodbody Newman isn't anywhere near here. You are. Give us the disc or we'll pick your carcass apart piece by piece until we find it."

"Where is she?" Mullet was just a blur through the blood that trickled down my forehead and into my left eye, but I could smell him. Both of them smelled like last week's trash. This time, Jeff did me upside the head from the other side.

"Nobody tol' you to ask no questions. Where's the disc?" he said. When I didn't respond, he set the .45 on the roof, grabbed me with both hands, and jerked me out through the passenger window like a string puppet. I hung there in his face, my lifeless deck shoes swinging an inch off the ground. "I'm gonna ask you one more time."

One more time never came. The hissing crackle of the CB radio erupted from the trunk. It was Stet's voice, asking where we were. By the time the trunk lid popped open, Mullet was already emptying his .38 special into the back of my car. Phil didn't have a chance.

Jeff just let go of me and reached for the .45. As I collapsed in front of him, I clutched his shirt with my left hand, and grabbed at the 9mm in his belt with the other. There wasn't time to do anything but flip the thumb safety and pull the trigger. We fell together, the big man with both hands clutching his privates and a real surprised look on his mushroom-nosed face.

On the other side of the car, Mullet was reloading. Lying facedown, my legs tangled up in the big man's, I looked under the car and saw six empty silver cases bounce on the concrete near Mullet's ankles. I'd seen this kind of view lots of times in the movies and always wondered why the good guys never shot the bad guys in the foot. I jerked the 9mm out of Jeff's pants and pointed it at the shabby brown shoes on the other side of my Camaro. Four missed shots later, I knew the answer.

Mullet's feet disappeared behind the rear left tire. Now, struggling to sit up, I tried to watch every conceivable approach route. Adrenaline pumped like gang busters through my system, but between struggling to stay upright, keeping the automatic poised at ready, and trying to get Jeff off my legs, the added energy just wasn't enough. And it didn't help to hear Mullet say, "You're dead. Dead just like the wiz kid we dumped in the river and dead like this hunk of garbage who screwed up my arm."

I was dragging myself toward the front of the car when Mullet made his move. It happened so fast I had neither the time nor the physical ability to do anything about it. The crater-faced sewer rat slammed the trunk and threw himself across it. The only thing I saw was his .38 special revolver. It appeared, spitting fire and lead, around the corner of the back window. We both emptied our guns, but a man's hand makes a worse target than his feet; and Mullet, with a bad arm, and without poking his ugly face around the corner, didn't know exactly where I was.

While I ejected the spent clip with my right hand and tore a full one off the holster strap, I heard Mullet's new empties roll off the trunk and bounce on the floor. I thought he might have shot Jeff several times, but a small wet tear in the denim above my right knee and a pool of bright red liquid underneath said I'd been hit too. Paralysis does have its advantages; I might bleed to death, but I wouldn't feel a thing.

When Mullet's cylinder clicked shut, I stopped dragging myself away from him, leaned back against the front right quarter panel of my car, and aimed carefully at the place where the deadly hand would appear. I prayed that he would stick his head out first and that my violent trembling might somehow enhance my aim. Both were tall orders.

My father always told me that God answers prayers.

"Sometimes, the answer is no," he'd say. "And most times, even when the answer is yes, it's nothing like you had in mind.

"But," Dad would go on with a dauntless glint in his eye, "God's answer—yes or no—is always best."

God's answer came as a great grunting eruption of force. Phil's snarling yell of exertion was accompanied by the explosive flinging open of the Camaro's trunk lid. That's what I heard. What I saw was Mullet's runty torso flipping helplessly through the air, bouncing off the roof of my car, and landing in a snarling, disheveled heap next to Jeff. Only when the 9mm automatic's slide locked open did it sink in that I had emptied the entire clip into the vermin's body.

I ejected the clip, replaced it with the last one on the holster rig, and dragged myself back toward the trunk. Jeff lay motionless, staring wide-eyed and clutching himself possessively. Alive or dead, he would pose no threat. Mullet wasn't moving, but his blood seeped out through more than a dozen new apertures.

"Phil?" I said, my hands slipping in the warm, pooling liquid. "Phil, can you hear me?"

There was no answer. I dragged myself around to the driver's door, threw it open, and struggled to reach the car phone. Police sirens now echoed outside, but Phil needed an ambulance. After ordering one, I yanked my wheelchair from the backseat and tried frantically to get into it. It was no good. Much of the sticky mess on the concrete floor came from a hole in my right leg. Pain or not, life's blood is life's strength. Finally, I altered my approach, climbing first into the lower driver's seat of the Camaro, then transferring into the wheelchair. I rolled back to the trunk, to Phil.

He lay still and silent, his gaping eyes glazed with the anguish and the effort of his final heroic feat, his blood shimmering around him like a dark pool of deep water. Jeff T. Thug was right about one thing. Heroes die in the real world.

I closed Phil's eyelids, took his hand in mine, and while my own blood ran down my leg and onto the floor of the storage unit, wept for all whose prayers of desperation have been answered.

$\triangledown$

1 8

I WOKE UP IN the hospital. My blue wheelchair was folded up against the far wall, and just outside the open door, a uniformed police officer drank from a Styrofoam coffee cup. My room's only window looked out over a wide ledge and across the city of Titusville. Seated by the window with one leg crossed over the other, reading a copy of the *Melbourne Sun Coaster*, was Agent god. His blue-gray three-piece suit had been cleaned and pressed, or perhaps he'd been issued a new one. The bruise on his right cheekbone was almost gone.

"Welcome back," he said, folding the newspaper and leaving his seat in the warm sunlight. "There's quite a menagerie of well- and not-so-well wishers waiting downstairs to see you. But I've got first dibs."

Great.

"We were never formally introduced, Mr. Foster. My name is Agent Stanley Fredericks, FBI. Everyone wants to hear about the great Titusville massacre," he said, taking a microcassette recorder out of his coat pocket and setting it on the bedside table. "Unfortunately, you are the only survivor. You may summarize for the others, but first, you'll spare me no detail."

The nurses tried unsuccessfully to convince the FBI man that I needed rest, so for the next two hours I watched the dripping IV bottle that was piped into my left arm, told Agent Fredericks my story, and answered his questions. Like any good reporter, I sought answers of my own. Serious law enforcement types are never easy to pump, but if you can make them think that they need to tell you something in order to get their job done properly, then it's all in the line of duty.

I learned that Mullet was really Anthony Spinoza and Jeff was Nicholas Ganto. They were on the outs with the mob in Miami, so took free-lance work wherever they could get it. The question remained—especially now that they were both deceased—who were they working for?

It seems that Nicky "the Nose" Ganto would have lived (albeit with a somewhat higher singing voice) if Tony "the Mullet" Spinoza hadn't shot him three more times. Tony, like Phil, never had a chance. Fredericks said he was sorry about my friend, but that the coroner's report suggested an instant, painless death from four bullet wounds to the chest. When I told him about the trunk lid, the diligent government agent just whistled under his breath and shook his head.

Along with numerous weapons violations, some obstruction of justice charges, and several "failure to comply" warrants, I would apparently have to answer "unnecessary violence" questions as well. The 9mm, at close range, made twenty-six holes in Tony the Mullet's body, the thirteen exiting wounds only slightly worse than those on the incoming side. "We call it overkill," Fredericks said. "Try telling the judge you were terrified."

No lie.

Randy White and Todd Gulick were next in line. With the aid of ten milligrams IV Valium, I was fading fast, but Randy wasn't about to let me out of his control again. He placed a small plastic suitcase on my stomach and started ranting like the true professional that he is.

"This lap-top computer is costing me two hundred and fifty dollars a week to rent, so you are not going to lie around here collecting workman's compensation and flirting with the nurses! It's got a forty-meg hard drive, and Todd's already programmed in your word-processing software and your current files.

"I'm giving the shoot-out feature to Todd—he's been doing all your work anyway—but I want you to stay on the shuttle thing. Whoever cracks the real sabotage story will make every paper on the planet. I want it to be us. Do you understand?"

"Thanks for asking, Randy. I'm feeling a little pain—you know, from the bullet wound and the pistol whipping—but the drugs help a lot. And how have you been getting along? You look a little pale to me—must be something you picked up hanging around the hospital."

"Don't give me that crap," he said, pulling a handkerchief out of his back pocket and holding it over his nose and mouth. "I'll shoot you myself if you don't get back to work!"

He started out the door, then turned back. "Did you really shoot the big guy in the zero zone?"

I just nodded.

"That's cold, Stick."

I fell asleep talking to Todd, but not before congratulating him on landing his first byline and thanking him for keeping mine alive. He filled me in on the various individuals we were watching and/or looking for. So far, nothing out of the ordinary was going on. I made him promise to keep hunting for information about Katie.

"Okay," Todd said. "I'll do what I can. Now, about the shuttle. They're talking September no matter what, but yesterday NASA cut through the *Discovery*'s outer skin in several places, supposedly to replace some type of 'valve.' My contact over there says the incisions she saw just happened to correspond to those locations throughout the shuttle, the main tank, and the boosters where the explosive charges are stowed. The destruct system is getting the fine tooth, Stick, but nobody's got a clue."

No kidding.

He told me he was taking care of Butkis and showed me how to use the lap-top, but that was all pretty fuzzy. The last thing I remember him saying was something about Randy paying for all Phil's funeral expenses . . . out of his own pocket.

When I woke again, the hospital smells were gone. My head was filled with the most wonderful mixture of fragrances: perfume, herbal shampoo, perhaps even a touch of pheromone. Even before I managed to open my eyes, I knew that other parts of me were already stirring. Then I felt the weight on my shoulder, heard the soft and rhythmic breathing, and realized that the satiny, scented hair was not part of my short, salt-and-pepper beard.

Sam's wheelchair was parked facing me, close against the bed rail. She slept peacefully, with her right arm across my stomach and the top of her head nestled gently against my face. I tried to lie still, hoping to make the moments last, but my nostrils fought for more of the intoxicating aroma and soon my chest rose and fell, drawing in ever greater volumes of the sweet-scented air.

"Careful," she whispered, turning to look in my face, "you'll hyperventilate."

"Let me worry about the danger," I said earnestly. "I want to face the peril and overcome it."

"You're so brave, Stick," Sam said, kissing my cheek before sitting up to stretch. "Too bad you don't know the difference between sunshine and shade."

Toast.

Sam filled me in on the fiasco that erupted sixty seconds after I pulled into the storage garage.

"When the signal died," she said, "Stet had everybody split up. We were less than a mile behind you, so we fanned out on all the side streets. Even when some of us thought we heard gunshots, nobody noticed the construction site until the cops started pouring in. Some lady on the back of the block apparently told them right where to go. Stet tried to keep in touch with everyone. He even tried your channel once."

"I know." I didn't tell her that was why Phil had died. Stet didn't need to know either.

When the night nurse finally figured out that Sam wasn't a patient, she booted her wheels right off the floor. I managed one last hug and sniff and thanked her for the company.

"I'll sleep on you anytime, Stick," Sam said on her way out the door. "Call me."

Like always, I promised I would.

$\triangledown$

19

"GOOD MORNING, MR. Foster. I'm Paul Waite," said the wizened man in wire-rim glasses and a white lab coat.

"Just call me Stick."

"The good news," the smiling doctor went on, ignoring me, "is that you'll live. The bad news is that you'll never walk again. But since that's real old bad news, and not my doing, I guess all the news is good." He winked and let go of my wrist. "Let's have a look."

The "in" wound, just above my knee, wasn't too bad— a small clean incision held closed with a half-dozen sutures. The bandage was dry and unsoiled. When the good doctor had me roll over, I could tell that the other side of things wasn't quite so neat and tidy. The sheets were spotted with seepage, the colors of which will never appear in anyone's fall fashion accessory line. When the sodden gauze came away, I lost most of my curiosity and stopped craning my neck to see.

"You think that's a mess," Dr. Waite said knowingly. "You should have seen it when I first got to play with it."

The bullet, a .38 special soft point, was apparently already mushrooming nicely as it passed through my leg— narrowly missing my femur and nicking the vein that wraps around behind the knee—and would have left an ugly exit wound under any circumstances. The fact that my leg had been resting on a semicured concrete floor added a whole new dimension to the fragmentation process.

"We had a friendly bet going in the OR," the doctor said, grinning mischievously. "You know, how many pieces each of lead, concrete, and bone? Nurse Butterfield won. She banked heavily on the concrete. How the bullet missed the bone, I don't know."

After checking the circulation in my right toes, Dr. Waite came around to the left side of the bed and started to remove a bandage on that thigh—one I didn't know I had.

"He shot me twice?"

"Um? Oh, no. Dr. Green and I gave you this one. Rather nice, wouldn't you say? At least tell Marty it is, you know, if he stops in to see you. He's so vain."

The shocking pink square was trying, with little success, to crust over. It had the soggy mottled look of a broiled salmon that's been on the buffet too long.

"We needed to borrow some skin," the doctor said, "to replace the chunk you lost underneath, over there. And since nobody in OR would volunteer any, we drew straws. You lost."

"Sounds fair to me," I said.

"Good. Now don't get out of bed until I say. If you rip up my nice work, I'll have all manner of nasty things added to your IV. I can't say what Marty might do, but I wouldn't chance it if I were you."

"How long do I have to wear this?" I said, holding up the board taped to my left arm, trying not to think about the needle that lay menacingly in my vein.

"Maybe a week. You lost a lot of blood. Now, be happy, don't worry, and keep relatively still."

Dr. Paul Waite left the room—a professional in his fifties,

mind you—singing "be happy, don't worry" and doing a walk
that was a cross between Bob Marley, Mick Jagger, and the
California Raisins.

When the nurses are not nursing, the doctors are not doc-
toring, and there are no sweet-smelling blonds asleep on your
shoulder, a private hospital room is a lonely place. I had been
pretty professional thus far, saying what needed to be said,
like a good reporter—the who, what, where, when, and why
of things. Now, in the solitude of my room, the ghostlike
faces of Phil Stilles and Katie Newman visited me often.
Sometimes, I thought maybe Jim Woods was there too, striv-
ing to get my attention. One way or the other, it all spelled
unfinished business.

   I was repondering all the ill-fitting puzzle pieces when a
nasty insight hit home. It was like realizing too late that you
misspelled someone's name . . . after the story went to press.
If, as Pastor Bob had told me, Katie Newman's folks died
when she was twelve, who in blazes had she called Saturday
morning from Burger Man?

   There are lots of rules in this life. Some of them beg to be
broken. Others—like reporters not getting personally attached to people in their more serious stories—can chew you
up and spit you out if you violate them. My objectivity had
been affected by a remarkable woman. I wasn't the first, I
wouldn't even be the last, but I felt like the stupidest.

   When I wasn't typing on the portable computer or using
the modem to tap into one of the data bases on Todd's seemingly inexhaustible list, I chatted with anyone who would
listen. All the well-wishers, assured that I would live, eventually went back to their jobs and their homes. I would have
called Sam, but being hoodwinked by Katie Newman left me
temporarily indisposed toward the emotions Samantha
Wagner was equally capable of eliciting.

   So I struck up conversations with the lower-rung officers

of the Titusville PD who drew guard duty at my door. While Stanley Fredericks had assured me the "precaution" was merely intended "to keep undesirables out," the men and women in blue soon made it clear that their instructions included strict orders to keep me in. They were all friendly enough; in fact, the Titusville Massacre was fast becoming something of a folk legend around the precinct. I soon found myself answering various technical questions about the shoot-out, much to the delight of my largely rookie keepers.

Despite the official police record, most of them had to hear firsthand about how I fired a 9mm round into Nicky the Nose's pants. Officer Mary Ellen Decker, while unconvincingly feigning embarrassment, made me tell it twice. When I asked her if she was planning something similar, she said only that she'd considered it several times. It was much easier to think of Mary Ellen as a "person" from that point on, but what does it matter how the lessons of antichauvinism are learned?

It was a Thursday night, and Mary Ellen usually drew the late watch at my door. Visiting hours were over, and the floor was settling into the long, quiet, lonely hours that are aptly known as the graveyard shift. It's a good time to work, if you're quiet and you don't get caught.

For some reason, nurses on graveyard at Titusville General tend to be underpaid (by their own reckoning), a tad surly (by most anyone's reckoning), and, on my floor at least, big. This last, and the accompanying intimidation it inspires, tends to make the bedridden patient think twice before asking for anything. I learned early on to get my toilet regime out of the way before the shift change and remain unnoticed, if possible, until morning. When the night nurse looked in on me, I always made it a point to be asleep until she was gone.

Anyway, on that Thursday night Mary Ellen was replaced by a short small-boned male officer with almond brown skin and jet black hair. Nurse "Broomhilda," the biggest of the big night nurses, sneered at him reproachfully as she goose-stepped through her lock-up rounds. When the echo of her footsteps died, he muttered something inaudible and glanced in at my bed. For some reason, I kept up the sleep act, peering carefully out of the barest slit between my eyelids.

"When it rains, it pours" was my mother's favorite cliché. It was about to pour. As Officer New Guy cautiously approached my bed, the moonlight coming through the third-floor, tilt-out window said: "Get out your umbrella."

Three things caught my reporter's eye. First, unlike any real rookie cop, my stealthy guardian's uniform was rumpled. Second, the silhouette on the moonlit floor behind him was that of someone else . . . someone outside my window. And third, barring an immense coincidence, the cop with the dark, thickly stubbled face probably didn't belong to the silver name tag with DECKER engraved across it. As it was my policy to leave Broomhilda strictly alone, I wasn't even sure where the call button was.

It wouldn't have mattered. The shiny curved blade appeared out of nowhere and plunged at my heart before I could even get my arms out from under the covers. Even as the knife struck the back of the hidden computer's flipped-down lid and I grappled for my attacker's arm, a second intruder popped out the screen and rolled in under the open window.

The man in Officer Decker's uniform was cursing me quietly in Arabic when the newcomer hit him from behind. The battle, though loud and violent, was short-lived. My third-story rescuer wiped up the room with the little guy, concluding the struggle with a groin kick that made me wince.

"Here," she said, flopping the groaning assailant across my bed as the sound of Broomhilda's running footsteps came down the hall. "I'll talk to you when the dust clears."

"Thanks, Butch," I said recognizing the fierce smile of the

lady who replaced the screen, slipped into the small wash-room, and closed the door.

Broomhilda called security. The battered Middle Eastern man was unceremoniously hauled away and a search for Mary Ellen Decker was initiated. The hefty nightingale relieved me of the damaged computer, saying I was as bad as her children, who, like all of us, had occasionally been caught with a comic book and a flashlight under the covers. She punished me by reinserting my IV.

Almost an hour later, after I had been questioned, a new police officer had been installed outside my door, and a badly beaten Ms. Decker had been found and admitted, I turned on the TV for some background noise and whispered to my guest that it was safe to come out.

"It's clean enough in there," she said quietly, "but there's nothing to read."

I wouldn't know.

$\triangledown$

20

BRENDA "BUTCH" GRADY, WHEN not tending bar, is a pretty talented free-lance private investigator. She's also one tough broad. Her sandy hair is buzz cut on top, feathered on the sides, and barely covers her collar. Steel blue eyes—like Glenn Close's—and teeth that flash when she smiles make Brenda a standout in any crowd. She is a black belt in karate, a first-class tri-athlete, and the only woman I've ever known who can hit a softball over the 285-foot sign on the left-field fence . . . just about anytime she wants.

"This is a dangerous place," she whispered, sitting against the wall on the left side of my bed, away from the door. She pulled up her knees and wrapped her arms around them. "I never knew it could be so much fun!"

"Not that I wasn't delighted to see you," I said quietly, "but what were you doing out there?"

"I'm working for you, Stick. Didn't Todd say?"

"I should've figured," I said, "the way his eyes glaze over when your name comes up, but why were you playing outside my third-story window?"

"They wouldn't let me in to see you—visiting hours and all that crap. Did you know that this place has a wheelchair accessible fire escape and a dandy ledge around each floor?"

"I do now."

"And you really don't know who that guy was?"

"No, I don't," I told her, "but that's only one of the things I'd like to make him talk about. I'll bet he knows Tony the Mullet and Nicky the Nose."

"Maybe we should have kept him for a while. I'd have made him sing," Brenda said, grinning. "If he even speaks English, that is."

Brenda had an unusual update on Martha Denton—just when I was ready to let Com-Tech's newly reascended computer queen off the hook.

"I couldn't get hold of Todd," she said, "so I thought I'd come up and give you the dirt in person . . . and see how you're doing, of course.

"Anyway, I was wrong about old Martha not having any friends. Turns out she has one extremely good friend, a Willa Perkins. I never saw them together because her friend lives in the next condo down the hall—and they have an adjoining door. When she's not sunbathing nude on the balcony, Martha's friend uses her own bedroom as a greenhouse."

"You haven't been engaging in a little breaking and entering now, have you, Butch?"

"Stick!" she said, rolling her cold blues up at me. "How could you think that about me?" Her teeth gleamed in the dimly lit room. "Didn't I ever tell you about my other business?"

"Pouring drinks and bouncing drunks?" The officer outside my door got up from his metal folding chair and looked in. I changed the TV channel—turning the volume up a notch in the process—waved, and nodded hello.

"No, not that," Brenda said when he had returned to his seat and his magazine. She handed me a business card. "I am also the proud owner of Delta Force.'"

The card said DELTA FORCE EXTERMINATORS, WE SEARCH AND DESTROY.

"Must come in handy," I said.

"Very."

While Martha's being a lesbian—in and of itself—wasn't grounds for suspicion, her roommate's hidden collection of newspaper clippings and Holcum antispace propaganda was.

"Wait a minute," I said. "What does Martha Denton look like?"

"Short, pale, mousy, and unsettled."

"I saw her at the funeral," I said quietly. "In fact, I saw them both. Is Tan Woman about six inches taller than Martha, athletic-looking?"

"Bingo. Quite a contrast, huh?"

"Mm. Anyway, speaking of bugs," I said, "can you do something about the U.S. Government-issue jobs at my place?"

"Sure! Can I keep them?"

"With my compliments . . . if not those of our good Uncle Sam. And, Butch, if you bump into Todd while you're over there, be kind. You know, a young man's first crush and all . . ."

Brenda raised an eyebrow and left the way she had come, slipping out the window like a graceful and muscular cat, pulling the screen into place behind her and promising to find out who Willa Perkins was and whether she might have something official to do with Senator Holcum. My unfinished business was getting more complicated by the minute.

I woke up to find Agent Stanley Fredericks once again reading the paper in my sunbeam.

"I hear you had an exciting night," he said, folding the *Sun Coaster* and sliding his chair over to my bedside. "I've got a few questions, as you might have guessed."

Surprise.

"We've identified the man who attacked you," he said nonchalantly. "At least one of his names is Arfaad. He's a holy warrior in the Islamic New World Jihad."

I'd heard of them—about a light-year to the right of the late Ayatollah. "Are they doing this on their own," I asked, "or are they Ben Holcum groupies?" The white hat in the three-piece suit actually laughed.

"It is rather convoluted, isn't it?" The smile looked out of place, and when Agent Fredericks sighed, I got a glimpse of the toll he paid to do his job.

"Anyway," he said, fully back to business, "I understand about the knife and the computer, but I'm pretty curious about how you clobbered the daylights out of him. The ER tech swears that you must have kicked old Arfy in the groin. Arfy's not talking."

I held up the IV splint on my left arm and waved it threateningly. "Any weapon in a storm."

Stanley Fredericks didn't look convinced, but let it drop. "The real question is: why?" he went on. "Why would our Middle Eastern friend roll a cop and sneak in here to get you? I took the usual precautions, but more because I wanted to know who comes and goes."

Stanley walked back to the sunbeam and left the implications hanging in the air between us. "Look, Mr. Foster, I know this would be a big scoop for you—"

"Call me Stick."

"—and I believe that's all you're after. But everybody knows that things aren't adding up real well. Even though Arfaad was probably only after some face-saving revenge this time, the only answer that makes any sense to most people is that Nick Foster still has the magical mystery disc, and would rather die than give it up."

He looked back at me from the window and shrugged. "But somehow that doesn't sit well either."

So, Agent god was human after all. "That's the way I felt about Katie Newman," I told him. "Now I'm not sure. But I'd bet my chair against Jim Woods having any willing part in whatever's going on."

"What is going on, Mr. Fo . . . Stick? What in the name of creation is going on?" He sat heavily in the chair and sighed again. "I keep seeing the *Challenger* blowing up over and over in my mind, knowing that if we don't come up with something in the next couple of weeks, it might happen again."

"And it won't be an accident this time," I said, sharing his frustration and finding it hard not to trust him. "I don't have it, Stanley."

"We've got Trish Taylor's copy of the program," he said. "We told her not to tell you, but it hardly matters. It's just like all the others, and every chipbrain we've got has been over it a thousand times. Still, I know that disc is somehow the key."

No kidding, Stan.

"Someday," he said, trying a friendly smile on his way out of my room, "when this is all over, you'll have to tell me who mugged Arfy. But I don't think it matters now. Oh, by the way," he added as an afterthought, "did they tell you Arfy had been shot before he got here?"

I looked up, startled, and shook my head.

"Maybe yesterday or the day before—right through the rib cage. Unfortunately for you, the bullet missed everything vital. It was a clean hole in and out . . . like a 9mm at close range."

Good grief . . . Katie!

"Take good care of him," I heard him say to the police officer outside my door. Then he was gone, leaving me feeling off balance. Did Stanley Fredericks, alias Agent god, really trust me? Or was I being set up by a seasoned professional? Upon reflection, I didn't really think that mattered much either, so I let it go and answered the phone.

"Hey, killer," said the whispered voice on the other end of the line, "they say you're my hero."

"We don't need another hero," I said. "Tina Turner told me that. Who is this?"

"This is Mary Ellen Decker, Mr. Foster. Thanks for getting him in the crotch. That was a nice touch!"

"Call me Stick. They said you'd been roughed up pretty bad. How do you feel now?"

"Rotten. But never mind about that, just give me all the gory details."

Some people.

▽

21

"THE POT'S BOILING NOW!" Todd said. He was breathing so heavily, I could picture the condensation forming on his telephone mouthpiece. "I mean it, Stick. NASA just canned Com-Tech after twenty years! No phaseout, no waiting until after the launch, nothing. Just abracadabra, and they're history . . . gone . . . I mean out to lunch . . . for keeps—"

"Okay, steady as she goes, Todd. Now start at the beginning."

"Stick, that is the beginning. I mean, I was having my little morning chat with Dave Bentley, and he says, 'Oh, by the way.' Stick? Do you hear what I'm saying? He says, '*Oh, by the way*, Com-Tech is out and Dynamic Industries is in. As of this morning.'

"This morning, Stick! Did you ever hear anything like it? What the heck does it mean?"

"Well, Todd, first it seems to mean that you're losing your professional cool. Finding out what else it means is our job. Your job. Now, if Com-Tech is gone, why was Dave Bentley still there?"

"That's another strange thing, Stick. Some Com-Tech employees were offered immediate positions with Dynamic.

122

Our friends Dave Bentley and Martha Denton were among the chosen few. What do you think?"

"I think you've got some work to do."

Todd rattled off the remainder of his notes: supposed hydrogen leaks on the shuttle, projected weather influences on launch scheduling, and glowing reports on Butch Grady. Before I hung up, I told him to ask Butch out.

"Oh, no, I couldn't! Why she'd never. . . . She's so, I don't know, *strong*. Oh, Stick, do you really think she'd ever go out with me?"

"Get a grip, Todd. Just ask her. She'll make a man out of you."

The search for Katie Newman was, according to federal, state, and local law enforcement officials, a nearly hopeless one. The Fonze personally worked overtime on it but came up empty handed. In the end it was Hector's cousin, Roberto, who found her—tied and gagged—in an abandoned Cocoa Beach shanty.

"Nobody has lived there for years," Roberto told me quietly while Hector looked on, "but it sometimes gets used for . . . international trade arrangements, if you know what I mean?"

"Mm."

"Anyway," he went on, "we heard there was some real out-of-town-type dudes camped in there, so we went to check it out. But when we got there, nobody was around but your *bonita chica*, see?"

"Yes, Roberto, I see. Where is she now?"

"I do not know." He was almost whispering, and looked over his shoulder at the cop by the door. "She says we are not supposed to tell nobody we found her . . . but you."

"You let her go!"

"Ssh!" Roberto said nervously. He cast a puzzled glance at Hector. "Hector says she is your girl, so we did what she says. Besides . . . she said it is what you would want."

Right.

They left, promising to look for her again, but they were both clearly confused. According to Roberto, Katie had a black eye and was hungry, thirsty, and soiled, but seemed otherwise okay. He said she took a small gun from a drawer in the shack's kitchen and had them drop her off at my place. My car, Hector added, had been cleaned up and left in the carport. After that, Roberto didn't know.

She wasn't at Phil's memorial service. It was held later that night in the hospital chapel, arrangements by Randy White. The place was packed out—mostly with ultralight orange wheelchairs. The team had only just met Phil Stilles, but that was enough. My orderly-escort rolled me down in a monolithic clunker of a wheelchair with a high back and an extended leg-support system designed to protect the good doctors' needlework. A five-foot stainless-steel pipe was mounted on the wheelchair's back frame, and my IV bag swung like Damocles's sword above my head. The whole mess weighed over a hundred pounds, while my own folding chair weighed less than twenty-five. Add to that the board taped securely to my left arm, and any thoughts of losing my keeper, rolling out the side door, and going home early were extinguished.

Phil's family consisted of a younger brother from Endwell, New York, and a married sister from Truth or Consequences, New Mexico. Both were shaken by the violence of their brother's death, but neither begrudged me my life. "Phil was always like that," his sister, Kathryn, said, taking my hand afterward. She was a short, attractive woman with strikingly intelligent and sensitive blue eyes. "He'd pound the living daylights out of any stranger who bullied Peter and me, but then turn around and take our lickin's for us at home, without a thought. Phil sent us clippings from your columns

about his business. The way he talked about you in his letters . . . he liked you a lot, Mr. Foster."

And I'd known him for less than a month. Sometimes life
is the pits.

"The realtor already found a buyer for the house, but we
need to sell his boat and all," Kathryn went on uneasily. "We
don't know much about that sort of thing. Maybe you could
help?"

"I'd be glad to help," I said. "I should have thought of it
before. Somebody has to run the traps, or pick them up.
They're already way overdue. The law says you can't leave
them untended for more than two days . . . cruelty to the
crabs I suppose."

"I can do it." Peter jumped in. He was a bean pole compared to Phil, but his eyes had that same easy sparkle that
made you want to trust him. "I've got some time coming at
work. I always meant to come down and go out with Phil."

The regret was heavy in his voice, but he seemed determined to settle up his brother's affairs. Somebody had to do
it, and I was temporarily indisposed. Maybe Todd would help
him in the morning.

"Where are you staying?" I asked them.

"We've got a room at a motel over on the Interstate," Kathryn said. "But I'm flying out of Orlando tonight. Peter could
keep my rental car, but he'd have to take me over to the airport."

"Why not use my car, Peter? You can stay at my house for
that matter. . . . I'm stuck here for a few more days anyway."

Kathryn and Peter were both grateful. Todd had already
gone, but Randy agreed to drop Peter off at my place. There
were spare keys, I told them, in the carport rafters, behind
an abandoned hornet's nest. He wouldn't need the broken
rake handle I used to put them there. Kathryn left for Orlando, taking Peter by their motel on the way. Randy promised to pick up Peter in the lobby at nine, and Peter said he
would call me when he was settled in at the house.

* * *

When I was ferried back to my room on the third floor and left alone with my call button and my scratched up mini-computer, I tried to sort through my feelings. First, I felt cheated. Phil and I had become good friends.

On top of that, I was homesick. I missed my house, my cat, and especially my waterbed. Everybody has some life routine into which they retreat when things get too hectic in the real world. Mine was a favorite reclining chair, any Harry Mark Petrakis or Dick Francis novel, any K. T. Oslin album, and a certain old brown Tonkinese purring nearby. Given those, I could lock the front door and escape from everything . . . at least for a while.

Literally and figuratively, the hospital stunk. I'd hated the smell five years before when another ambulance delivered me to another hospital, and I hated it now. They all smell the same. I had lots of cards and letters from friends and readers this time, and that helped some, but the loneliness and the loss of freedom were just as depressing when the long sterile night descended on the quiet corridors. No, at least this time I knew what lay ahead for me personally: my wound would heal, they would return my wheelchair, and I would go home, back to being a newspaper writer. Maybe I'd finally write a novel.

Five years before, after being told that my lower back was broken and my spinal cord damaged irreparably, I didn't have a clue what to expect. I found out soon enough. The girl I'd been planning to marry slipped uneasily out of my life, long-time friends, visibly ill at ease around the wheelchair, found various reasons to fall away, and my father died of cancer. "Hang in there, Nick," he said the last time we talked. "God's plan for you doesn't depend on your being able to walk. If it did, He wouldn't have allowed this to happen!" It all came back to me with the lonely smell of my hospital room.

My mom died when I was still in high school, so I'd grown real close to my dad. After his funeral, I'd left Orlando and moved to Melbourne. His insurance check, after funeral and burial expenses, provided the down payment on my small house and paid for several writing courses at the Brevard County Community College. I made new friends who, like Phillip Stilles and Randy White, hadn't known me when I surfed and played racquetball. They accepted me, wheelchair and all, for who I was . . . and I started over. There were a few old friends, like Hector Heeta, who still made a place for me in their lives, but it would never be the same.

While I turned on the computer and the telephone modem, I thought about Sam Wagner and the Orlando Orange Wheels. Shortly before I'd been discharged—while I was still wallowing in doubt and self-pity—Sam rolled into my Winter Park hospital room. After introducing herself, she checked out my injury level and started into twenty questions: did I play ball? Was I a guard or a forward? Was my free-throw percentage any good? Did I have a steady girlfriend?

"Not anymore." My simple answer to all of her questions was cold and surly. It was, in retrospect, intended to make her go away and leave me alone. Or, at the least, to make her feel sorry for me. She just laughed.

"It's pretty crappy for a while," she said on her way out of my room, "but it gets better if you work at it hard enough. When you get yourself together, maybe I'll show you my tattoo!"

Despite myself, I spent that night fretting less about poor me and wondering more about Sam Wagner's tattoo. The thought of someone that good-looking in a wheelchair was curious at first, but then I realized that I'd always gone out of my way not to look at anyone in a wheelchair . . . a habit I broke in a hurry when I learned I'd be living in one. Some prejudices just sneak up on you.

Almost every day after that, someone from the team

showed up in my room or found me in the therapy gym. They just talked to me. They told me about hand controls for my car, modifications to make my chair lighter and faster, and what wheelchair athletics was all about. The day I got out, Joe Stetler took me out to lunch and let me drive his '85 Camaro . . . and of course I had to have one. Two weeks and two basketball practices later, Sam showed me her tattoo.

The Wheels often went out for pizza and beer after practice. On those nights, the local Pizza Den found itself up to its ovens in wheelchairs. It was only my second time going with them, but as the sole cola drinker in the crowd, I had already been voted the team's chief designated driver.

On that particular Friday night, long after the joint would normally have closed, Sam Wagner and Eddie Stiggins got into a beer-drinking contest. I could never tell who was winning, but I knew they would both be losers in the morning. When it was over (a pretty sloppy and inconclusive ending), Joe Stetler offered to take Stiggy home, and I was assigned Sam Wagner.

She made it to my newly modified blue Camaro all right, and after I helped her into the passenger seat, I loaded her chair into the trunk, my chair into the backseat, and drove away. On the way to her apartment, Sam laughed for a while, told me several story fragments, and then inquired as to whether she'd ever shown me her tattoo. I'm sure it had nothing to do with my being "together," it was only because she was more than sufficiently apart, but while she fumbled with the buttons on the front of her blouse, I tried, but not too hard, to keep my eyes on Orlando's deserted city streets.

Of course city streets are rarely deserted—they just look that way. I don't know how many blocks went by while I watched my passenger's fumbling fingers more than the white line on the pavement, but the flashing lights and the brief wail of a siren brought my voyeuristic attention suddenly back to job one. It was far too late for that though. Just before she passed out, her shirt wide open to the early morning Florida air, Sam laughed one last time and said, "Just show him my tattoo."

The computer screen fluttered to life, giving me a prompt for my instructions and bringing me back to the task at hand. I keyed the number of an on-line news service data base and skimmed the listings for details about the shuttle program, Senator Ben Holcum, and the Islamic New World Jihad, but discovered nothing that Todd had not already told me. There were warnings about a "Trojan horse" virus on several of the local computer bulletin board services that Todd belonged to, and I made a mental note to ask him what that meant. The phone rang as soon as I disconnected the lap-top computer from the phone line. It was Peter Stilles, and he sounded pretty rattled.

$\bigtriangledown$

22

"IT WAS TERRIBLE!" Peter said. But I thought I heard laughter in the background.

"What's going on?"

"Randy dropped me off at your place," Peter said, "and I was attacked."

"What? Are you all right?"

"Just barely!"

Now I was sure I heard laughter.

"Stick? Are you still there? I opened your front door, see, and this real tough lady tossed me across the living room like a bean bag. Then this other lady shoves a gun in my face. You're missing a heck of a party. Here, somebody else wants to talk to you."

Peter passed the telephone and Hector's Latin tenor voice came on the line.

"Everybody is here but you, amigo. How is the leg?"

"Okay," I said, wondering how Butkis was handling the unscheduled company. "What's going on there? Did you find Katie?"

"Sure, Nicholas," he said, "right where we left her. You want I should let you talk to her?"

"Yes, Hector. Thanks."

They were playing my Moody Blues tapes on the stereo. I could hear "Ride My Seesaw" in the background.

"Hi, Stick."

Katie's voice made me shiver. I was glad to hear it, but very confused about . . . everything.

"Hi," I said. "What are you doing there? Are you all right?"

"I'm fine. I was sleeping—oh, I love your waterbed—anyway that was before this place turned into Grand Central Station. First it was your friend Brenda. She took out a dozen bugs and told me about your encounter with Arfaad. Isn't he a sleaze? It's too bad I didn't shoot straighter. I could've saved you and Brenda—oh, and that poor cop too—all the trouble."

"But—"

"Then Hector and Roberto came back. They just kind of hung around to watch TV. Then Todd showed up to feed Butkis. He stayed to watch Brenda, I think."

"What about the police?" I said, wondering why Katie wasn't in custody.

"Oh, they're here too," she assured me. "Officer Sanchez stopped by on his way off duty to see what was going on, and we sent him for pizza. Just about the time he got back, Agent Fredericks and Agent Lopez arrived."

"But—"

"Oh, yeah, Sam rolled in with Joe Stetler and some of the Wheels, and then Randy White showed up with Peter, so we sent him out for more pizza and put Peter up to the phone call. That's about it. It's kind of an unofficial wake, I guess."

"I guess so," I said, more confused than ever. "How's your eye?" It was all I could think of.

"Brenda says it looks like I've been punched out by an Orc. What does that mean?"

"I'm sure I don't know," I said. "Let me talk to Stanley."

"Who?"

"Agent Fredericks."

"Ah." Katie put the receiver down and I listened to the new Moodies sing "I Know You're Out There Somewhere" while Agent god came to the phone.

"Mr. Foster? Nice party."

"Stick," I reminded him. "Thanks."

"I suppose you're wondering. . . ."

No kidding.

It was all over. Agent Fredericks didn't sound convinced to me, but officially, he said, the great cloak and dagger, computer tampering, murder, and kidnapping case was closed. Arfaad was locked up (probably forever . . . thanks to Butch); Mullet and Jeff (who worked for Arfaad, kidnapped Katie, and had admitted killing Jim Woods to both Katie and me) were dead (thanks to me); Katie Newman had been "rescued" (thanks to Roberto); and the shuttle had been declared safe for launch (thanks to Dynamic Industries and their star computerhead, Martha Denton). The End.

It seemed almost too obvious, but I asked Stanley about the missing disc.

"I don't know," he said thoughtfully. "That's the only hole in the cover of the closed file, the way I see it anyway. Katie said it wasn't in your cat's litter box—she was rooting around in there when Mullet and Jeff nabbed her. Since everybody wanted it at the end, we figure it's safe to assume that nobody had it. Still, we wish we had it."

"If that's the only hole you see," I told him, "you're way ahead of me. What about Holcum?"

"What about him? He's a zealot, but we couldn't link him to any of this."

"And what does Ms. Denton say was done to the computer program?"

"Nothing. They test that software every time somebody

gets up to go to the water cooler. On several receivers, just to be sure."

"What?" I said. The whole synopsis made everything seem like a bad dream. "Why are four people dead then?"

"Try this: Jim Woods thought he'd make a fast buck selling Mr. Arfaad the program. . . . What harm would it do? He got cold feet and died of it . . . with the disc—unbeknownst to Mullet and Jeff—in his back pocket. Arfaad's people probably just wanted to use the disc to screw up the shuttle . . . slap the American devils in the proverbial face. According to the folks at Dynamic, they probably couldn't have done anything with it anyway. But they didn't know that, and Arfaad was paying Mullet and Jeff big bucks to find it. Once word got out that you had it—"

"Thanks to my tireless public servants, the Federal Bureau of Investigation . . . ," I said, interrupting.

"Sorry," Stanley said. "We're still trying to figure that one out. Anyway, enter the three musketeers—Nicholas (alias Stick) Foster, Phillip Stilles, and Katie Newman. The rest is history."

"I don't buy it," I told him.

"I didn't think you would. One way or the other, the *Discovery* flies again the week after next."

Good night, nurse.

I sent Stanley back to the party, asking for Todd Gulick.

"I was just about to ask Brenda to dance, Stick. Could you make it quick?" he said.

His excitement, and his anxiety, radiated through the phone lines. I told him about Phil's boat and where to find the key. He promised to take Peter out in the morning.

"Clean out the crabs and bait wells," I said, "but leave the traps out there. I'll call the patrol tomorrow. Take the live crabs to Giovanni's—they'll give you fifteen cents a pound."

"Anything else?"

"Yeah, Todd. What do you think of Agent Fredericks's explanation of things?"

"I haven't heard it."

"When you're through dancing, get him to tell it to you.
Then come over here tomorrow sometime and let me know
what you think."

"Okay. Can I go now?"

"Good-bye, Todd." Sweep her off her feet . . .

I hung up, thoroughly confounded by the sudden cessation
of mystery—at least as far as the authorities were concerned.
As always, the tiny compact laser disc raised the biggest
question marks—question marks that, for me, weren't likely
to go away anytime soon. If it wasn't in the litter box when
Katie got there, where was it? Obviously Arfy's gang never
got it. Stanley Fredericks and the governmental good guys
claimed never to have laid eyes on it. And Propjob sure didn't
sneak into my house at high tide and take it back. He wasn't
that kind of dolphin.

The second biggest question mark was Jim Woods. I'd only
seen the young man once, and that memory was a grisly one.
But over the past couple of weeks, I felt I'd come to know
him pretty well. Pastor Bob McClarrin may have missed a
note or two on Katie Newman's sheet music, and he probably
wasn't alone, but he knew Jim Woods's tune by heart. The
"Woods sells out" theory just didn't work for me at all—despite the convenience to all concerned.

And what about Katie Newman? There were several unanswered questions in my mind: who was she really? Was
she mixed up with Senator Holcum? Who did she call on
the phone the day she was kidnapped? And, was I in love
with her? I guessed I'd have to sleep on that one for a
while . . . alone.

$\triangledown$

2 3

AFTER SEVERAL MORE DAYS of therapy—stretching the stiff and tender knee which, fortunately, I couldn't feel—they let me go home. Doctors Waite and Green were both delighted with their work and took pains to threaten me about taking it easy for a few weeks. I promised not to roller-skate, play touch football, or get shot again, and that seemed to appease them.

No charges of any sort were filed against me, and Joe Stetler's weapons were returned to him without a hitch. Thanks to Agent Stanley Fredericks, Uncle Sam agreed to pick up the tab for the body work on both Joe's Monte Carlo SS and on my leg. In addition, several local police departments went together on a good citizen plaque, in honor, I suppose, of my interesting combat stories. Mary Ellen Decker proclaimed herself at my disposal should I ever need help from the Titusville police. I told her I'd keep her in mind in case I ever wanted some guy kicked in the crotch. Her smile gave me the shivers.

Peter was still living in my small guest room, but Katie Newman had come to the hospital, kissed me on the cheek, said "Thanks for everything," and flown back to Kansas City. Just like that. When I got home, I found that her essence—etched in my memory for all time—still clung to my pillowcase. Butkis seemed to share my dissatisfaction at the abruptness of it all, but neither of us were in a position to do much about it one way or the other.

When he returned from his morning out on the Intercoastal Waterway with Todd, Peter Stilles informed me that he was quitting his job as an assistant archivist for IBM in New York and taking over his brother's business. He offered to pay me rent for the third bedroom until he could get a second job, but I said he could work it off by helping with the house and yard work.

I went back to crabbing, both to finish the story I had begun and to help Peter get started. I didn't think the good doctors would appreciate me dragging my newly repaired leg down the length of the dock, so I let Peter help me in and out of the pilot's chair. Getting out on the water again was good mental therapy. Unlike my cat, I love the salt air. I introduced Peter to Propjob and they got on at once.

"In a magazine, I think," Peter said with enthusiasm, "I read about a place in the Keys where you can actually swim with dolphins. I mean they don't make them do tricks or anything, you know, by withholding food, but you can get in the water and if they take a shine to you, you can play around with them. Wouldn't that be something?"

I'd heard about that research facility too, and Peter's remark turned on my inner light switch. "That might make a good story," I told him. "I think I'll look into it."

Randy rubber-stamped the idea and I made reservations with Dolphins First in Key Largo for a week in the spring. Everyone went back to their lives, but when several of us gathered at the cape to watch the *Discovery* launch, it was clear that things were not satisfactorily settled in any of our minds.

The weather was beautiful and the launch went off according to schedule. Peter came with me, and we met Todd, Brenda, and Jerry and Sam Wagner at the same oceanside park where Katie and I had our talk with Dave Bentley. Watching the great bird trace its graceful arc-shaped escape from the atmosphere was, at first, unsettling. Long after the bird disappeared from sight, and the radio in my car assured us that everything was perfect, we all sat around the gnarled picnic table wondering why we weren't more relieved.

"It's eerie," Brenda said as the white vapor trail began to break up. "All that fuss . . . and now, nothing. I don't care what they say, Martha Denton doesn't sit well with me. Neither does Tan Woman. Are you sure you don't want me to dig around some more?"

"I'm not sure at all," I told her, "but until I can justify the expense to Randy, that story's on indefinite hold."

"I don't understand the Com-Tech, Dynamic Industries switch thing at all, Stick," Todd put in. "Dave Bentley—and everybody else—says it was just time for contract bids and Com-Tech took too much for granted, but it smells fishy to me."

"Morton does a lot of that," Jerry said. "Sometimes they'll plan on taking several years' worth of loss, just to steal a contract from a firm that's been getting fat and lazy on the job. The timing with Com-Tech, though, is odd."

"You said Trish Taylor had pretty much figured out Jim Woods's program," Sam said to her brother. "Tell us what it does, exactly."

"The work performed is simple," Jerry answered. He opened his pocket notebook on the picnic table and twisted open an expensive-looking gold pen. "This is the shuttle—or any launch vehicle for that matter. Over here, here, and here are the range safety officers. Some of them might be flying, while others watch radar screens on the ground. All of them, I would imagine, are authorized to send destruct signals to any or all of the explosive packages aboard the various flight components."

Jerry drew three square buildings on the ground of his illustration. "These are the transmitters. I don't know where they are exactly, but I assume that they're spread out along the escape trajectory—maybe one here at the cape, one partway down the Florida coast, and one in the Keys or the Caribbean.

"Now, say the shuttle's doing fine, but one of the boosters goes haywire after being jettisoned and heads for Miami. This RSO in the chase plane," he said, pointing at his picture, "spots it, determines that it's leaving its approved flight trajectory, and pushes the appropriate destruct button. His radio sends a signal to the computer on the ground and Jim's program takes over, telling the appropriate transmitter to send the right message to the receiver in the booster. Got it so far?"

We all nodded.

"Okay, so, according to Trish, that message will be a series of tonelike transmissions, the length and frequency of which are coded to the appropriate charges. The computer-receiver on the booster recognizes its signal and sets off the explosives . . . BOOM! No more booster."

"It doesn't sound all that complicated," Brenda said.

"Maybe not," Todd broke in, trying hard to make a good impression, "but it's the timing that's hot stuff. Right, Jerry?"

"That's right. Once the button's been pushed, the whole procedure—thanks to Jim Woods's parallel processing technique—takes less than a second."

We just stared at Jerry's picture and tried to comprehend how all that could happen so fast.

"Dave Bentley says they've gone over Jim's parallel processing with a fine-tooth comb," Todd said. "And he seems to think that Martha Denton would have loved to find a flaw in the boy genius's technique. Nothing. Besides, the signals are tested constantly, right up until moments before launch. If the test telemetry doesn't come back *exactly* right, they just won't launch."

Mm.

*   *   *

The shuttle was back in business. Two months later, the *Atlantis* carried another payload into orbit without so much as a hint of trouble. In March, the *Columbia* went up . . . flawlessly. Katie Newman sent me a note that same week, saying she had some time coming, and could we "do something together?" I had pretty well reconciled myself to the fact that my jumbled feelings for her were one-sided and that I had no reason to expect that our time together meant anything more to Katie than it was . . . a nasty adventure in the aftermath of her fiancé's murder.

Now she wanted to come to Florida for a vacation. With me. She suggested May, so I wrote back and invited her to join me in Key Largo. Swimming with dolphins suddenly sounded even more romantic. But then I was letting my mind run on again.

In the real world, living with Peter turned out to be an experience all in itself. The skinny young fellow with decidedly book-wormish markings turned out to be something of a renaissance man. His knowledge encompassed a wide range of subjects—music, art, business administration, to name but a few—and his ability to get things done efficiently verged on remarkable. He sold his car by telephone, "arranged" to have his meager belongings packed up and added to the back of someone else's moving load, and, in less then a week, was a Floridian. Because of economic necessity, he sold his brother's sprawling house along with most of the furnishings, but not before disassembling "my" ramp.

After collecting his brother's tool chest at the local Ford dealer, Peter set about tuning up everything in sight. When his inherited pickup truck, my Camaro, my riding mower, and his Mercury outboard were all running even better than before, he started closing in my carport.

"If I'm going to keep all these tools here," he said, "I'd better make the place a little more secure. I'll build a workbench along the back wall that's the right height for you. I'll use a stool."

*   *   *

Peter had his brother's touch with junk, and my new garage soon had its own electric door opener, a rejuvenated discard salvaged from someone's weekly trash pile.

"If you don't like having a garage, I'll tear it down when I move out," he promised.

I liked it just fine.

His flare for organization was no less impressive. In a matter of weeks, my comfortably frumpled house was a model of organizational efficiency. Everything had its place, but fortunately, whenever I failed to get in step with the program, Peter picked up after me without a word. Only my desk was sacrosanct; Peter knew without needing to be told. He wasn't nuts about it or anything, but Peter was definitely a tidy kind of guy.

Thursday became wash day. Maybe it was some kind of creation ordinance with Peter, I don't know, but unlike my system of waiting until there was nothing left to wear, dirty clothes always turned into clean ones on Thursday night. I joked that the laundry room could be his office, and Peter actually thanked me.

"There'll be plenty of room for my computer stand," he beamed, "if I just move things around a bit! Here! I'll rig a swinging door into the garage for Butkis and ship the litter box out there. You don't use these overhead cupboards anyway. . . ."

He was rearranging his new "office," moving the dryer to the wall by the door, when he insisted that I come see what Butkis was doing.

"I thought you'd get a kick out of that," he said when my jaw dropped.

There on the newly exposed linoleum floor, surrounded by gray lint balls, odd socks, and other bits of memorabilia from years past, Butkis was busy playing paw hockey with himself. I'd seen him play the game many times before, but never with that golden puck.

$\triangledown$

2 4

T HE LASER DISC DIDN'T belong to me, of course, but then everyone else had already written it off for lost. Peter agreed that it was a fitting souvenir—considering what we'd all been through—so we decided to keep its resurrection to ourselves. As I turned the disc over and over in my hand, I willed it to yield up its secrets. Nothing.

On the floor next to where Butkis had secreted the missing computer disc, I found the folded top page from Jim Woods's notepad. That, at least, was a perfectly normal victim of laundry day. It was embarrassing to have forgotten all about it, but the sentimental doodles hadn't held any clues that I could decipher. I opened it up and rescanned the scribblings before wrapping it around the laser disc, securing it all with rubber bands, and asking Peter to put the enigmatic package in the garage rafters with the spare keys.

My weeklong report from a portable concession stand on New Smyrna Beach wrapped up uneventfully. Ben and Marty Mayfair had bought the small trailer with part of their life savings and, in 1982, retired from Trenton, New Jersey, to the quiet community with its drive-on beach. New Smyrna is about twenty miles south of Daytona and draws a more laid-back crowd than that famous racetrack and spring break town. Ben and Marty graciously danced around my wheel-chair, letting me try every phase of the business, from grilling hot dogs and hamburgers to changing out the soda fountain machine. If a guy liked the ocean, the heat, and an endless parade of bikini-clad women, it might make a nice career.

Meanwhile, Peter took to crabbing as though he were born to it. He quickly discovered three new (and cheaper) bait suppliers and talked about buying nets and catching his own bait at night. When he found out that new traps cost over twenty dollars each, he promptly took one of Phil's apart and used it as a pattern to build more. "A whole roll of galvanized chicken wire," he told me, "doesn't cost much more than that." He took me into my new garage one day and showed me the first three traps off the workbench assembly line.

"They're pretty," I told him. "But what's the yellow-green stuff?"

"Zinc chromate paint," he said proudly. "Ships use pieces of zinc on their rudders and keels to inhibit rust. Some crabbers even wire a small chunk to each trap. I thought a light spraying with zinc chromate might do the same thing at a lower cost. We'll see. . . ."

"So how many traps will you have in the water by June?" I asked. While blue crabs can be harvested year-round, June starts the season, a two- or three-month period in which crabbers can expect to catch two to three times as many crabs in each trap.

"Two hundred, I hope."

"Do you miss the archives sometimes?"

"No way!"

While I tried to study up on marine mammals for my May assignment in Key Largo, some internal clock counted the moments until I would see Katie Newman again. I went crabbing with Peter on most mornings. I practiced, and occasionally warmed the bench, with the Orange Wheels. I even joined in at the Orlando Pizza Den. But all the while, the mental ticking echoed in the back of my mind.

"Earth to Stick Foster. Come in."

"Huh? Oh, hi, Sam."

"Your pizza's going to grow its own toppings if you don't eat it soon."

"Thanks for sharing that pleasant observation."

"You're seldom what I'd call the life of the party, but this business with Katie Newman's coming has got you spacing between galaxies."

"How did you know? I mean, I didn't tell any—"

"Your Katie did." Sam slid a folded piece of Katie's stationery across the checkered plastic tablecloth. "She wrote me first."

"Why?"

"Stick, Stick, Stick," she said, shaking blond hair back off brown shoulders. "I know you're not really stupid, but sometimes I think you're as dense as a Florida basement. Maybe you've never figured out how I feel about you, but Katie knew right away."

"Sam, I always thought, well, you were just—"

"Teasing? Flirting? It used to be that, Stick, and I'm sorry. I think having Ms. Newman around made me think it all through." She looked down at the table and then back into my eyes. "I haven't been with anyone since before you were shot—not even a date."

"I didn't know—"

"It's the talk of Orlando!"

"I'm from out of town," I said weakly, knowing at once that the retort was a mistake. "I'm sorry. That sounded flippant."

"I used to think you were just a prude," Sam pressed on, oblivious to anyone else's presence in the room. But now I know that's not right. I think you're looking for the stuff of sonnets and love songs, Stick."

Listening to Sam paint wings and a halo on my emotional insecurities was almost unbearable. Only the thought of stopping her so I could explain was worse.

"I think I love you, Nicholas Foster. And if I don't seem like the type of woman a man would write sonnets for—"

"Sam! It's nothing like that."

"—I always want to be your friend. Even if all you need is a hug."

She withdrew the note, which had remained folded on the table between us, and rolled away.

"Nothing in life is ever easy," my Dad used to say. "If it is, you probably shouldn't ought to be doing it."

Mm, thanks, Dad. I feel much better now.

The *Atlantis* went up and came back again without mishap in early May. Agent Fredericks's official summation was looking more and more plausible, though it still didn't sit easily in my heart. If, however, someone were in a position to disrupt the shuttle program, letting it continue so smoothly with its busy work schedule seemed counterproductive.

On Wednesday, May 24th, I rolled nervously up and down outside the gate area at the Miami International Airport. The nonstop from Kansas City was due momentarily, and I was woefully distracted. Sam had been sending me weekly "friendship" cards, while Joe Stetler and Eddie Stiggins took turns chiding me about breaking her heart. Sam and I did dinner and a movie several times, but both of us worked too hard to keep everything on a safe, light level. I learned much more about her life "before," and about her progress at Stetson, and began to see Sam Wagner in an all-together new light. But each time I left her, I told myself that her infatuation with me would surely wear off soon. Only then—if she was still serious about settling down—would she find the *right* someone.

When I looked up, streams of disembarking passengers were overflowing into the outer gate area. From my artificially lowered vantage point, I couldn't keep up on the newest arrivals from the rearmost seats in the 727, which now loomed just outside the plate-glass window behind the check-in desk. While people embraced one another all around me, I gingerly jockeyed my wheelchair toward a more open stretch of the gray-blue carpet, and strained for a glimpse of Katie Newman's fiery red hair.

"Are you looking for someone in particular?"

I knew the voice at once, but the strong fingers kneading my knotted shoulders from behind were, if heavenly, new acquaintances. In the next several seconds, I mentally blocked out all of Miami . . . everything but the massage and the voice. I think I tried to say "hello."

"Why, Mr. Foster, I believe you're purring!"

"Call me Stick. Mmmmm . . ."

$\triangledown$

25

KATIE TOSSED THE FAMILIAR carry-on bag into my trunk and we made our escape from Miami. After the warm greetings, our brief silences seemed strained. I don't know what I expected, but Katie Newman wasn't acting like a carefree graduate student on a late but well-deserved spring break. She asked and answered all the right questions, but some unseen obstacle stood between us. My thoughts turned to James Woods, and I reminded myself that whatever else might happen with Katie and me, the late computer wizard would never be far away.

I almost told her several times about finding the laser disc but always held back at the last second. I don't like pregnant pauses. Silence is bad enough when one is alone, but even then I run the stereo to block it out.

"Katie," I said, finally, "can I ask you a couple of questions?"

"Sure, Stick. Fire away."

"Did you go to another school before the University of Kansas?"

"Sure. I graduated from Geneva College. Before that I took two years at JCCC—Jefferson County Community College."

"County? Not Parish?"

"Of course, county. Watertown, New York. Jefferson County. Why?"

"Oh, it's just one of those unanswered mysteries from the past. Can I ask you about your folks?"

"Of course you can, but what's this all about?"

"Just things I need to know. You said you were calling your folks that day when we went to the dog track before the trade for Sam's brother. Bob McClarrin told me that your folks died when you were twelve. Who were you really calling, Katie?"

"You're a thorough little reporter, aren't you, Mr. Foster?" Katie said with a grin. "I knew that the FBI suspected me, but I didn't know I was on your list too."

"It's not like that," I said feebly. "I was just wondering."

"Ren and Phyllis Catloth are like parents to me. I met them when I first got to KU, and they just sort of adopted me. They live a few blocks off campus and treat me like one of their own kids. Ren was going to give me away at the wedding. I even call them Mom and Dad."

Even though I thought there was some hurt showing in Katie's eyes, I was glad I had asked. I hate being suspicious. I really needed to know. Before either of us could say anything more, the phone rang.

"Stick?"

"Yeah, Todd. What's up?"

"You won't like this much."

"I can take it, Todd."

"Arfy's out."

"What do you mean, 'out'? He's out of prison? I thought he was gone for all time."

"Nothing lasts forever. Some of his friends stole a helicopter in Topeka, dropped into Leavenworth, and popped him out. They killed eleven people doing it."

The idea was staggering. The FBI convicts this terrorist on enough charges so that he'll never see the outside world again, they spirit him away to an "undisclosed penal facil-ity," and after a few months, poof, he's free . . . and eleven more people are dead.

"Stick? Are you still there?"

"Yes."

"That's not even really the bad news. You want I should save the rest for another time?"

"No, Todd. You're on a roll already. Go for it."

"Well, it's about your house. Or rather, what used to be your house."

"My house! What about my . . . Todd, is Peter okay?"

"Yes. He's right here. I'll let him tell you."

Peter sounded so jazzed it might have been funny . . . if it had been somebody else's house. I pulled off the road and parked the car.

"Man, Stick," Peter said, breathless even before he got started. "You should have been here! Agents Fredericks and Lopez showed up this afternoon, all in a huff, and told me that I was moving out . . . fast! They only let me take a few things, so I grabbed Butkis and the computers. I hope there wasn't anything else?"

"My sports chair?"

"Sorry."

"Crap."

"I . . . ah . . . did get a few of Butkis's toys though—"

"Great, Peter! You leave a twenty-two-hundred-dollar wheelchair . . . and salvage the cat's toys?"

"Well, you know how much he loves the catnip mouse, and, ah, his new hockey puck?"

Sam Wagner was right. I am dense sometimes. "I'm sorry, Peter," I said quickly. "You did just fine. Tell me what hap-pened?"

Katie leaned over close to the cellular phone and listened in while Peter, who was interrupted often by Todd Gulick, told a bizarre tale that wouldn't have sounded so far-

fetched . . . if only it had come from one of our Middle Eastern embassies, and not my modest three-bedroom house in
Melbourne, Florida.

"It was a pretty simple plan," Peter said. "I'm just glad
Agent Fredericks anticipated something. One of Arfaad's
buddies stole Betty Crenshaw's car while she was in the gro-
cery store, filled it with explosives, and while the feds
watched your house, looking for an outsider, he rigged it to
drive through Don and Betty's carport, your fence, and the
back wall of the living room."

"Good grief, Peter. Was anybody hurt?"

"No, but there's hardly a window left on the block, or across
the street for that matter. Your house is mostly just gone."

"When the jihad gets pissed off, they really get pissed off,"
I said, trying to envision the damage and comprehend the
reason behind it. "What do we do now?"

After I hung up, Katie and I just sat, parked under a banyan
tree, and stared at the swamp grass beyond. It seemed safe
enough to assume that the James Woods computer-tamper-
ing case was now reopened, but with the shuttle program
running like proverbial clockwork, what could account for
the tenacity of the personal attack on me? The answer, as it
had from the beginning, remained hidden somewhere on
Butkis's new hockey puck. I would have to tend more seriously to that upon my return. My return to what?

"You found that computer disc, didn't you?"

I focused back suddenly, realizing that Katie had divined
Peter's little secret message.

"Well, yes," I said. "It just sort of turned up. Butkis had
it squirreled away behind the clothes dryer."

Katie considered me seriously, watching my eyes. "You
couldn't make that up," she said finally, "even if you were
capable of a half-decent lie!" Her laughter was as warm as
the Florida sun. "So, do we follow the plan?"

"Well, we'll sure forget about the Holiday Inn," I said. "But otherwise, I've still got a story to write. Randy's sending Butch down in the morning, so at least we won't have to look over our shoulders all the time. I'll understand if you'd prefer to make new vacation plans. I can run you back to the airport."

"No way!" Katie said with a pained look. "There might be a real answer or two to come out of all this yet. Besides, I've kind of missed the excitement . . . and you, of course."

Yes, ma'am.

I pulled out onto the highway and left the mainland behind. Crossing onto Key Largo is always a kick, because there is something magical about seeing the Atlantic on your left and the Gulf of Mexico on your right. It's like that all the way to Key West. There, of course, you can also see the Straits of Florida. Oh, it's all the same water—only our maps define the distinctions—but there is something mysterious about the Keys. Traveling from bridge to bridge along that curving archipelago is like visiting another country. Key West even attempted a tongue-in-cheek secession in the early eighties; I have a framed Conch Republic flag hanging in my living room . . . or at least I used to.

$\triangledown$

26

I SAW IT ON the right. The sign said SEAFARER RESORT MOTEL, and there was a wooden statue of an old fisherman, dressed in yellow rain slicks and holding a ship's oil lantern. The driveway wound back through the palm trees and palmettos, so that I couldn't even see the office from Highway 1.

"This place looks pretty secluded," I said, turning in through a break in the decorative coral wall that ran the length of the motel's road frontage. "How about a couple of cabins on the gulf?"

"How about *one* cabin on the gulf? I'm on a budget. And it's not like we haven't shared a motel room before."

Yes, ma'am!

Frank and Loretta Adams owned and operated the Seafarer. They were "retired," according to Frank, who had proudly served the state of Ohio as a highway patrolman for thirty-five years. Loretta just rolled her eyes and said, "Maybe *he's* retired, but I've never worked this hard in my life! But," she added quickly, "it's worth it . . . just not having to worry about whether Frank will be coming home in one piece every day." I'd seen the statistics. Nationwide, state highway patrolmen experience one of the highest percentages of work-

151

related fatalities in the law enforcement community.

Our cottage—with its knotty pine–paneled walls and its sixties decor kitchenette—sat next to the motel's gulfside beach.

In the blossoming orange sunset, it was hard to imagine that someone had blown up my house. Or that my life was in jeopardy. Katie and I chose two of the well-padded wooden lounge chairs and sat in silence for nearly twenty minutes, watching the great fiery ball sink slowly into the Gulf of Mexico.

"Terrorists kill people," I said, at the very same instant Katie said: "There's something I have to . . " I missed the rest.

"What?" We both asked at once.

"You first," I said.

"No, you," Katie insisted. "You said something about terrorists?"

"Terrorists kill people," I repeated reluctantly, realizing that I hadn't really intended to say it aloud the first time.

"You're a quick one, Stick," Katie said. "How long did it take you to come to that learned conclusion?"

"What I mean is, Arfy might hate me for getting him beaten up and locked up. He might even have paid Mullet and Jeff to kill Jim and nick the laser disc. But why would he and his buddies want to screw up the shuttle program? What religious or political motivation would they have? When there are so many creative ways to kill hundreds of innocent men, women, and children, why go to all this trouble to target a shuttle crew of five or six or seven?"

"Who knows?"

Katie shrugged her shoulders, kicked off her Reeboks, and walked to the water's edge. I watched her draw in the wet sand with her big toe, her body silhouetted against the darkening horizon . . . a sight not particularly conducive to serious deductive reasoning. I climbed back into my wheelchair and rolled out on the floating dock, past the pedal boats, to the scale-covered fish-cleaning counter. Even the faint smell of dead fish is better when mixed with the warm salty tang of night air on the gulf.

"I've got it!" I spun the light chair around so fast I nearly rolled off the edge of the dock. Katie looked up from her sandy artwork. "How do you kill lot's of people with something like the space shuttle?"

"You don't," Katie answered.

"Unless," I added with feeling, "it falls out of the sky on top of them!"

"You mean instead of trying to blow up the shuttle—"

"That's right! Everyone assumes that the bad guys want to deliberately blow up another shuttle, but what if they just wanted to keep NASA from being able to operate the self-destruct system? Sooner or later some shuttle—or its booster rocket, fuel tank, etc.—is going to stray off course. And what if the new course is toward Daytona or Miami. Or the cape? The perpetrator doesn't have to do anything. Doesn't even have to be in the country. The trap is set, it's unnoticeable unless we figure it out, and it's the last thing anybody expects!"

"It's certainly a novel idea," Katie said thoughtfully.

Novel? Good night, nurse.

I rummaged around in the Camaro's console box until I found Agent Fredericks's nondescript business card and used the car phone to call the number. Just like he promised, when I told the dispatcher who I was, she said he'd call me right back.

"Sorry about your house," Stan said when I answered my phone. "We never really expected anything quite like that, but I thought it might be a good idea to move Mr. Stilles."

"You mean you knew I wasn't there?"

"Well—"

"Oh, never mind, it's to be expected, I guess. Thanks for warning Peter."

"Just part of the job," he said. It might even have been a

shot at humor. "By the way, Lopie, I mean Agent Lopez, says you haven't checked into the Holiday Inn yet. Are you okay?"

"No one will ever accuse you of not being thorough, Stanley," I said. "Yes, I'm staying at a little out-of-the-way place. Tell the little guy that he can have my room at the HI. Randy already paid for it. I assume that he knows where I'll be tomorrow?"

"That goes without saying."

"Yes, of course it does! Look, Stan, I think I may have hit on something worth looking into, but talking on this radio rig probably isn't a good idea, is it?"

"No, it's not," he said seriously. "Call collect from a pay phone. I'll tell the dispatcher to expect your call; you give her the number. Ten minutes?"

"Got it."

Katie wasn't anywhere in sight when I hung up. I figured that she had gone inside. The jalousies on the cabin's front door were open wide, so I shouted in, telling her that I was driving up to the convenience store to use the pay phone. I left my wheelchair sitting there by an overgrown and sweet-smelling gardenia bush, pulled myself the rest of the way into the Camaro, and followed the winding driveway back out to Highway 1.

Stanley Fredericks admitted right away that my idea was an alarming new possibility, and he seemed quite disappointed that it had not occurred to him first. He promised to look into it, asked me to be careful, and then, just before hanging up, told me to hold on.

"I shouldn't be telling you this—it's definitely off the record. Will you keep it to yourself?"

I told him I would.

"Stick, the agency has been interviewing witnesses at the airport in Topeka and at the Leavenworth penitentiary." He paused, as if uncertain whether to go on.

"And?"

"And there might be something funny about the 'terrorists' who sprung your friend Arfaad. Almost all the witnesses—thirty-three, I think—said they saw a helicopter full of heavily armed Middle Eastern types. You know, dark mustaches, scarves, the works. But one older black inmate told us that the terrorists were Afro-Americans and white guys, *made up* like Arabs."

"Mm."

"Think about it," Stanley went on. "How often have you heard of Middle Eastern terrorists showing up in full ethnic regalia?"

"You mean like Arfy in my hospital room, for example?"

"Exactly."

I used the drive-up phone to call Jerry Wagner and Todd Gulick. Both promised to retool using my new scenario. Jerry thought it a far more likely idea, at least from a computer programming point of view, and said that he and Trish Taylor would look over the program again. Todd was, well, different.

"Look, Stick," he said, "I'm sorry about your house and all, but I've got my own assignment to write; I can't do your column this time."

I hadn't even asked.

"That lap-top and modem will let you dump the stuff right on Randy's desk . . . from anywhere."

"I know."

"And, uh, when Butch gets there tomorrow, I hope you'll be careful. I mean you should kind of look out for her, okay?"

I almost reminded him that Butch Grady was being paid to look out for me, but something in Todd's voice made me think better of it.

"Sure, Todd," I said instead. "No problem."

"Good," he said firmly. "I'll get back to you."

I just hoped he wouldn't forget me when he reached the top.

* * *

Back at the Seafarer, I pulled up to my lonely looking wheelchair and started to climb out from behind the steering
wheel. A great white gardenia blossom rested on the chair's
seat cushion, and there was a piece of folded paper attached
to the right brake handle, stuck there with a tiny wad of
chewing gum. When I was safely on board, with the aromatic
flower sitting on my lap, I opened and read the terse note.

> Stick,
> I had to leave unexpectedly. Sorry. Thanks for every-
> thing. . . .
>   Katie

$\triangledown$

27

THE ROMANTIC GULFSIDE CABIN was suddenly cold and lonely. Infuriatingly, it still smelled like Katie Newman, but as I sat at the laminated table in the small kitchen and hammered out the next day's column, my anger burned slowly away, leaving an even greater intellectual curiosity about the mysterious woman, and no small amount of chagrin at having been a fool. Again.

When I put down the car phone after uploading my work to the *Sun Coaster*'s sleepless computer, it rang immediately.

"Stick?"

"Hi, Peter. What gives?"

"I've been pondering that piece of yellow notepaper, and there's one doodle that doesn't seem to fit in with the other lovey, huggy, stuffed bear graffiti."

"Really?" I thought I had looked the page over quite thoroughly. "What's that?"

"Well, it's just a scribble, but it might say: 'ComDat 5.0.' "

"Does that mean anything to you?" I didn't remember seeing any such thing.

"ComDat is a sophisticated software program put out by the Download Company in Chicago. It's designed to look at two other programs, compare the programming data bit by bit, and note any differences."

"Yes! Peter, you done good! How long will it take us to find a copy of ComDat 5.0 and get it to Jerry and Trish?"

"Well, Stick, there's the rub, so to speak. Download is constantly upgrading the program; but so far, ComDat 4.0 is as far as they've gotten. Even in the development lab they're only working on version 4.2. I called this afternoon."

"Mm. Maybe Jim Woods just wrote it down wrong. We'll get Jerry the 4.0 version and compare the two programs on the disc."

"Stick, listen, I'm already working on that, but neither of them can legally do something like that at Morton. Can you think of some other way, or, more specifically, some other *place*? It's probably another dead end, but I think it's worth a try."

"I do too, Peter. It's too much of a coincidence to be a dead end. I hope. I'll get right on it, and thanks. How's Butkis, and where are you staying, by the way?"

"Butkis is still a little unsettled, but well enough. We, you and me and Butkis, are now the guests of Melbourne's own Marina Club Motel. I got us a two-bedroom unit with a kitchenette. It's all wheelchair accessible, and your home owner's insurance is picking up everything. Is that okay?"

"That'll work fine, Peter."

"Something else, too. I spent a couple hours going through the wreckage with the Fonze and the insurance adjuster. Lot's of our stuff is okay. It got blown all over the place, and the delicate things broke, but there wasn't any fire to speak of, and most of our clothes, your books, even your other wheelchair, just got buried in the rubble."

"Well, that's good news, anyway. Thanks a lot, guy. We'll sort it all out when I get back."

"Oh, I've already done that. I rented a temporary storage locker here by the marina and arranged everything that was salvageable by amount of dirt and damage. I'll start washing on Thursday."

I should have known. I made two additional calls before turning in, readied my camera for the morning, and went to bed wondering about what might have been. Somewhere, not too deep inside, I knew that I was relieved. At least about one thing. A romantic evening with Katie Newman—whoever she might be—was a grand and beautiful thing to daydream about, but when I thought seriously about how it might actually have gone, some of the dreamy luster faded. I just wasn't ready. The timing just wasn't right. And anyway, the woman just wasn't here anymore. So long, and thanks for all the fish.

The next morning I considered canceling out on the dolphin story, but some inner programming urged me to follow through. There wasn't much I could do about the other mess at the moment anyway. As it turned out, I almost didn't find Dolphins First at all. The address meant nothing to me, and even on the tiny island of Key Largo, I had to ask four residents (two of them service station operators) before someone thought they knew where the secluded research facility was located. Unlike the other dolphin "research" locations in the Florida Keys, Dolphins First made no effort to advertise. While restaurant and motel lobbies boasted boatloads of colored flyers promoting other dolphin shows, DF seemed almost too low key.

As I drove into the graveled parking lot, across from the nondescript complex enclosed by a chain-link fence, Butch Grady approached my car casually, only after carefully, yet nonchalantly, scanning the area for hidden boogie persons. It would have been funny if the recent events in my life had been other than what they were.

"Hi, Stick Man!"

"Hi, Butch. I see the marines have landed."

"You bet. Where's Katie?"

"Long story. The bottom line is: she's gone."

"I see," Butch said, one eyebrow rising slightly. "Well, sorry . . . I guess. Anyway, from now on, you don't know me, you don't notice me, you don't even venture a glance in my corner of the compass. Got it?"

"I guess so, but remember that Agent Lopez is around here someplace. Don't maim him or anything; he's just a tiny guy after all. And about looking—well, Todd is right, Butch. How can I resist those startling baby blues?"

"Oh, shut up."

Yes, ma'am.

Butch wandered off and I climbed into my chair and headed for the front gate, trying not to think about my baby-sitters. It was time to consider the man who made Dolphins First tick. Danny Baxter made the change of subject easy.

"You must be Nick Foster," he said, extending his hand. "It may be a year or two more before we can think about blacktop; but you know, *dolphins* first! Can I help you through that gravel?"

"No, but thanks," I said, surprised at how naturally he responded to my disability, falling in step alongside. Most folks just reached out and started "helping," whether I wanted help or not. "It's good exercise," I said. "And please, call me Stick."

Danny Baxter didn't miss a beat.

"Okay, Stick, look. The first group starts its lecture in fifteen minutes. I've got you down for the afternoon group, like you asked. You can sit in on either lecture and take pictures whenever you like."

"First I'll ask you a few questions," I suggested. "Then I'll do the lecture thing, then how about I shoot the morning group during their swim time?"

"That'll be fine. Let's get to it."

Danny Baxter, not surprisingly, watched *Flipper* as a child. He "fell in love" with dolphins then and never grew out of it. After studying marine biology and working at several sea aquarium-animal show facilities, he grew increasingly uncomfortable with the way the gentle mammals were being treated.

"If they don't perform, over and over, on cue, their food is withheld. They're forced to interact with humans whether they want to or not. That kind of relationship causes stress, which in turn can cause the animal's premature death."

Danny Baxter's facility, I learned quickly, was clearly not intended as a tourist attraction. Those who sought out Dolphins First made reservations months in advance and traveled from all over the world to experience earth's most graceful mammals up close. They did so for many reasons, but Danny Baxter sought earnestly to turn them all into "dolphin disciples."

Danny had set up his own model of how man should study dolphins without endangering or enslaving them. The ground rules were short and simple. Guests at DF *never* reached out to touch a dolphin. They were, in fact, admonished not to pursue the gentle creatures in any way. The animals had to make the first move, an invitation that obviously indicated they wanted to be touched. Even then, the ever-present staff of marine biologists had to confirm the "message" and give the guest permission to respond.

When the morning lecture began, I set my microrecorder on the red picnic table in the small thatch-roofed pavilion by the "pens." Pens is not a very accurate term, at least not in the way we usually think of pens. The chain-link enclosures were obviously not intended to keep the dolphins in, as even the youngsters could easily jump over the top. They were to protect the creatures from the boats that came and went through the canal that bisects Key Largo and opens into the Atlantic.

"At lunchtime," the lecturer said, "we open the underwater gates and let the dolphins out into the canal. The Atlantic is less than a thousand yards away, and these dolphins are free to leave—then, or anytime. We think this helps relieve some of the stresses that real captivity can create. Leaving them with all the choices about things that affect their lives is as important to them as to us."

I started to tune out, enjoying the looks on the faces of the other listeners. They were, Danny had said, two very different groups of people. Half of them were undergraduate students in marine biology from the University of Southern Florida. The rest were from the state mental facility at Chattahoochee.

"We've been working with the disabled on almost every level, since the beginning," Danny had said. "The dolphins seem particularly drawn to humans who are, well, different. And they often help shy, insecure, and withdrawn individuals to come out of their shells. One blind youngster came here afraid of everything and almost everybody. His therapist called me two weeks after their visit and told me that she and the boy were going rock climbing."

While I was photographing the group, it struck me that the lecturer had just said something significant. She was talking about dolphin sonar, but I would have to play the tape back later to find out what I'd missed.

$\triangledown$

28

SWIMMING AND PLAYING WITH Atlantic bottle-nosed dolphins is an experience that is so strangely moving, even a good reporter has difficulty describing it well. At least that's the excuse I used at first. By the time I'd left the gulfside cabin's kitchen table and rolled out on the dock for air and inspiration five or six times, it occurred to me that I was just plain distracted. I decided to watch the very last signs of daylight disappear from the sky and listen to the morning's lecture tape. That would, I hoped, get me back into the necessary work mood.

Butch Grady's Chevy Blazer was parked at the next cabin up from the beach, but I hadn't seen her proverbial hide nor hair . . . not that I was looking, of course. Orders are orders. Some sixth sense told me that wherever she was, Butch Grady was laughing at my obvious lack of concentration. The microcassette machine droned on quietly while I relaxed on the oversized lawn furniture and watched the stars come out. Alone.

I dozed off, I think, but something snapped my attention back to the tape recording. It was that sonar business again. I rewound the tape a few counters and started it again. What

I heard was a voice from above, light dawning after a starless night, a revelation that I felt certain would unlock at least one of the puzzles I was facing.

"Come, children!" I shouted to the surrounding flora and fauna as I climbed back into my wheelchair. "We're going home now."

I left the cabin key on the kitchen table, threw my stuff in the car, and honked the Camaro's horn on my way past the Adams's office. In my rearview mirror, just before I wound my way back to Highway 1, I saw Butch Grady tossing things in the red Blazer, rushing to keep up with her charge. Though I couldn't see him, I knew that Lil' Lopie was somewhere nearby doing exactly the same thing. And he probably liked it even less.

Getting around Miami would be a little slow, but then I was going to fly all the way to Orlando. Maybe I could use the national security thing if I got stopped. Maybe Lopie would take care of it. Who was I kidding, Agent Lopez would probably stop and testify against me. Anyway, car phones are wonderful, especially when you're in a hurry.

"Dave, buddy, pal-o-mine! Did you find that little item I asked you to look for?"

"Foster? Is that you? It's—" There was a crash in the background, presumably Dave Bentley's alarm clock. "It's, ah, late. Can't this wait?"

"No, Dave, it can't."

"Well then, yes. I found it in a storage room on the second floor."

"Good. Now be a Boy Scout, and go and get it for me. Okay?"

"Go get it! It's the middle of the night, Stick!"

"Now, Dave. It's not even eleven-thirty."

"You gotta be kidding. There's a predawn military launch tomorrow morning. I have to be there at three!"

"Great. You can just stay there, catch up on some

paperwork, drink some coffee, and you won't even have to worry about getting up!"

"You're nuts. Besides, security won't even let me walk out of there with a company pencil."

"Mm. Okay, I'll take care of that. Just be ready to bring it downstairs when security pages you. Got that?"

"Look, I don't have to do any of this."

"No, Dave, you don't. The way I see it, there's some good guys and some real bad guys mixed up in this. And the authorities are having lots of trouble figuring out who's who. But this might help them make up their minds about Dave Bentley."

The line was so quiet, I thought for a second that he'd gone.

"All right," he said quietly. "I'll do what you say."

My next call eventually woke Agent Fredericks.

"This had better be as good as the last one, Stick."

"Better. Look, Stanley, can you pick something up over at the cape and meet me in Orlando?"

I told him what we needed from Dave Bentley, and he agreed that now was better than later.

"Oh, by the way," he added before hanging up, "we questioned the folks in your neighborhood again. The 'Middle Eastern' man seen getting into a moving minivan just as your house blew up was probably a white guy."

Mm.

It was a good night for waking people up. I woke Meghan Wagner, who woke her husband, Jerry—but only after my slightly exaggerated assurances that the FBI was behind it all. Jerry reluctantly agreed to wake Trish Taylor. Gene Woods was really out of it when I called, but eventually, with some coaching, remembered my earlier call.

"Can I have some coffee ready for you all?" he asked sleepily.

"Thanks. And I'm sorry about the time. I didn't plan to come this soon."

There was a short silence when I told him how many of us were coming, but he finally assured me that it was no trouble.

Todd Gulick wasn't happy at all. At least not until I reminded him that Butch Grady would be there. "And bring your modem," I added quickly, "and that computer bulletin board system list you showed me too." Todd, still a shade grumpy, said that he'd be there as soon as he could.

Peter Stilles was last, but not least.

"What about pizza?" he suggested between yawns. "I can stop on the way."

"Good idea," I said. "We'll make it a mystery party! But don't stop. We'll order in."

Without a space shuttle launch in the near future, the prospect of unraveling the puzzler with plenty of time to spare was a festive concept. Except, of course, for the fact that someone was still very upset with me, as demonstrated by the house that was no more. Even so, maybe the Great Orlando Mystery Party was destined to be the place where that individual would be discovered as well. I'd never attended one of those mystery dinner affairs I'd seen advertised, but now that I was acquiring a more pronounced taste for the subject, I vowed to make a story out of the next one I heard about.

$\triangledown$

29

DESPITE WHAT WAS SURELY a world record drive from Key Largo to Orlando, everybody else beat me there easily. Well, except Butch Grady and Agent Lopez, that is. Butch and I parked end to end down the now-crowded street and headed back to Jim Woods's cottage only to find that the driveway was still empty. The rest of the gang had also parked curbside. Lopie didn't pull in behind us. My guess was that I'd lost him going around Miami.

Todd, Peter, and Butch carried my wheelchair and me up the cottage's four front steps, and Gene Woods, still in his bathrobe, placed a mug of steaming coffee in my hand.

"You're on to something, aren't you?" he asked. There was hope in his eyes.

"I want to think so," I told him, "but we'll just have to wait and see."

Jim Woods's bungalow was built in another era. It might just as easily have been constructed in a deep, dark European forest. It had Hansel and Gretel written all over it. Brown timbers, white stucco, and mossy cedar shake shingles graced the outside, and the front room, with its soft, antique furnishings and small, welcoming hearth made the visitor feel at home. The house felt perfect for a writer, or maybe a professor. It also gave off the sensation of loss and emptiness, despite the fact that it was currently filled with people.

The party began to take on a more constructive mood when Trish and Jerry managed to successfully connect the laser read-write unit that Agent Stanley Fredericks had commandeered from Dave Bentley.

"Got it, Stick," Jerry announced proudly. I excused myself from Gene Woods and wheeled over to the largest of the late computer wizard's three terminals.

"Where's the magic disc?" Trish asked without looking up from the keyboard.

Stanley fairly rose up into the air and hovered over me. Agent god returned suddenly from the great beyond. "The disc? You told me you didn't have the disc!"

"Well, I didn't and I did," I answered lamely. "I mean I did, but I didn't know I did. Peter?"

Peter handed the golden circle to Stanley, and the FBI man turned it over and over in his hand and shook his head slowly while I explained.

"So this is it," he said reverently. "Can you do something with this that you couldn't before?"

"That depends. Peter, did you find the ComDat thing?"

"You bet! It was just like you said, too. Tell him Trish."

Her fingers danced on the plastic keys. "Jim Woods took the basic program apart six ways, and when he was finished putting it back together, it was twenty-five times better than the original . . . and twice as fast. It'll take the Download people five years to catch up to what he's done here. If they ever do."

I couldn't help noticing the look of pride on Gene Woods's face. For my part, clearing Jim's name and nailing the head rat in this maze had gotten very personal.

"He could have been a rich man many times over," Peter added, "if he'd gone the commercial route."

"Well," Trish said, looking up for the first time, "it's ready to run. Are you going to tell us what we're looking for?"

It was time. I prayed that my brainstorm made as much sense to the experts as it had to me. Suddenly, as I was about to be tried and sentenced for my theory, the idea didn't seem quite as foolproof as it had in the Florida Keys.

"Okay," I began, "it's like with dolphins. They talk to one another in clicks, lots and lots of clicks. It's some kind of sonar. Well, the marine biologist at Dolphins First said we have a long way to go before we learn to translate it, or understand exactly how it works for navigation, but the experts think that when whales and dolphins get caught in shallow water or washed up on beaches it's because a virus of some sort screws up the sonar signals. Get it?"

The faces around me remained blank.

"Well, look, Todd recently gave me a minicourse on computer viruses, specifically the Trojan horse variety that has been going around. If I understood you correctly," I said, looking at Todd for confirmation, "they look just like legitimate programs, but they have a trigger or a hook that sets them off sometime after they've been loaded into a system. Like after a certain number of times the software is run, or even on a specific day, date, and time.

"What if our saboteur has access to a computer chip manufacturing facility and a way to get in and switch out the chips at NASA? From the army of thugs we've seen so far, it's obvious that he or she has no cash-flow problems. And what if the secretly replaced ROM chip had both the correct program on it *and* a 'hooked' program that would automatically replace the right one on a specific day at a specific time?"

Jerry jumped up from the seat next to Trish Taylor. "Yes!" he shouted. "I see it! There's a story going around about a launch several years back. One of the guidance programs turned out to have a capital T in one of the value tables instead of a lowercase one, and when it was time to set the rocket's orbit, they tried to run the software and it crashed. The rocket just kept going. If somebody altered the program too far ahead of time, every computer jockey at NASA would notice it right away. Have it switch automatically, *just* before the launch, no one but the computer would ever notice."

"Until it was too late," Stanley added soberly.

"You may have something," Trish said, a growing smile lighting up her face. "I'd never have thought to look for that. But you might as well relax. Even running ComDat's souped-up compare program will take a while."

As the party guests took up the theory and excitedly tossed it around, my hopes rose. Todd, I noticed, was busy at the Macintosh SE computer on the adjoining breakfast counter.

"Well, Todd," I said to Melbourne's rising star cub reporter, "any luck?"

"I think so. The BBS you asked about is the Panthers, and you remembered right, it's sponsored by something called the NASA Headquarters Information Technology Center in Washington. I've got the number here, and I just have to create a dial service on Jim Woods's communications software. What was it you wanted to ask them?"

BBS is short for bulletin board system. On the surface, it's almost like a computerized CB radio club. People from all walks of life and every corner of the globe join these electronic networks and exchange messages, debate all things great and small, play games, and meet new friends—all from their bedrooms, family rooms, or home offices. Most BBSs list General as their area of interest, but some specialize in games, "adult" subjects, science fiction, fantasy, etc. The BBS from Todd's list that had caught my eye when I was in the hospital heralded its affiliation with NASA and listed Computers and the Space Program as its area of specialty.

"Two questions, Todd. First, what is the backup plan in the event of a failure in the fail-safe destruct system? I presume it's navy jets or some such. And second, which shuttle has the shakiest mechanical record? That is, if they were going to have a Panthers BBS pool on which launch vehicle was most likely to screw up on its own, which one would those in the know be most likely to bet on."

"Got it," Todd said. "You realize that the sysop won't likely be around at this hour—at least not awake—so I'll probably have to leave a message. I can check back tomorrow to see whether or not anybody wants to be helpful."

"Go for it, guy. And thanks!" The sysop, or system operator, is the boss or manager of a given BBS. The board runs on the sysop's computer, and all of the network members communicate by sending their input to and receiving their answers from his central command location. In the world of BBS, the sysops are gods. One plays by their rules, or one does not play.

"You know," Trish added, "anybody with enough money and influence to do what you suggest could probably pay someone to jimmy with the launch vehicle as well. You know, just some minor compromises to systems that may already be trouble prone. Might better their launch-specific odds significantly."

Mm.

I noticed that Butch and Stanley were confabbing in the small kitchen. When he saw me looking their way, Stanley motioned for me to join them.

"We're comparing notes on Martha Denton, Arfaad the Awful, and the mysterious Katie Newman," Stanley said when I made my way to the small hardwood breakfast counter. "Your friend Brenda seems to know quite a bit more than we do about Ms. Martha."

"*Hypothetically*," Butch said quickly. "I'm only speculating on what one *might* find if one were to examine the condo of someone *similar* to Martha."

"This Tan Woman, Willa Perkins, is a new one to me," Stanley said, laughing at Brenda's disclaimer. "Her name hasn't come up anywhere. I was about to try running her through my computer in the car. She can't generate any less data than Katie Newman."

Stanley started to rise but never made it to his feet. The sound of an engine, roaring at maximum rpms, filled the heretofore quiet night air, and the even louder BOOM, BOOM, BOOM, BOOM, BOOM of semiautomatic gunfire punctuated the immediate sense of danger. The explosion that followed blew out the windows and shook the late Jim Woods's cottage like a paint can in an electric stirring machine.

$\triangledown$

30

"EVERYBODY OKAY?" STANLEY shouted. He scanned the room while running for the front door. "Stay down!"

I had no choice. I lay sprawled on the floor, covered with both broken glass and Butch Grady. She'd swept me out of my wheelchair and onto the floor as if I were a feather, and shielded me from further danger. When she was confident that I was alive, Butch lifted her body off mine and headed for the now-open bay window.

"The earth moved for me, Butch!" I said as she got up. There was a trickle of blood on her face.

"Shut up!"

"Was it as good for you?"

She disappeared into the night.

The rest of us lay there and picked broken glass out of our clothing and our bodies. Everyone was bleeding from at least one cut, but no one seriously. The silence was quickly too much for me, and despite the scolding of my fellow grovelers, I climbed back into my chair and rolled to the front door and out onto the small concrete porch. A lone shot rang out, and before I realized what had happened I flew out of the chair and landed in a disheveled heap, four steps down on the sandy lawn. Stanley Fredericks whirled out of the nearby shadows, his automatic scanning the front yard.

"It was just one of my high-pressure tires, Stan," I said. "Glass."

"I told you to stay put!"

"Sorry."

The FBI man was all business now, and he quickly disappeared back into the shadows. Halfway to the street, on the lawn to the left side of the driveway, was a totally demolished automobile, trying to stand up against a palm tree whose top had been blown away. The make of the car was anybody's guess. I heard voices in the bushes where Stanley had gone and the faint sounds of sirens in the distance. Knowing I'd add chigger and sand burr damage to that of broken glass, I dragged myself across the lawn, past the smoking wreck, and into the darkness beyond.

"They were right about these 10mm automatics," said a struggling whisper of a voice. "Couldn't have done that with the old .38 specials." There was a spasming, liquid-filled cough. "Sorry I didn't get it . . . before it got this far, but . . . it came out of nowhere. Is anybody hurt?"

"Shut up, Lopie. Save your strength. You did real good, and everybody's fine. If you hadn't shot out the tires that crate would have rolled straight up onto the front steps and killed us all."

"It hurts, Stan."

"I know. Just hang on. The medics are almost here."

As my eyes grew accustomed to the darkness, a grotesque scene unfolded in the bushes before me. Stan was Stanley, but the short man whose hand he held could have been anyone. Anyone, that is, run fully dressed through a meat grinder and tossed into the palmettos. Agent Lopez hung there like a broken and bloody corpse, his shoeless feet dangling a foot off the ground.

"Get the guy who did this, Stan," he whispered. Then he coughed up more blood and died.

*   *   *

Needless to say, the sleepy Winter Park neighborhood was
now fully awake. People in bathrobes crowded around the ambulance, the police cars, the fire trucks, and the mess. After
Steve Lopez was taken away, Stanley took control of the situation. Agent god was back, and no one questioned his authority. He ordered the local police to disperse the sightseers,
he sent the fire truck back to the station, and he urged the
second team of paramedics to patch us up and go away.

Peter Stilles and Edna Woods, who, fortunately, had not
been in the cottage when the car bomb exploded, handled
the trauma with house cleaning. The two of them—kindred
spirits—talked in hushed voices while they helped each
other sweep up broken glass. Jerry and Trish returned to their
compare project in silence, and Todd went back to the BBS.
Butch Grady had disappeared into the night and not returned. Gene Woods paced around the outside of the small
house, muttering something about plywood.

I got the paramedics to hand me my crippled wheelchair,
then climbed in and headed down the street toward my car.
I had several spare inner tubes, a screwdriver, and an old blue
bicycle pump in the trunk. The poor chair listed hard to starboard, but I limped it out of the driveway without mishap.
As I passed the demolished car bomb, I thought I smelled a
hint of pepperoni pizza. So as the last of the police officers,
med teams, and firepersons disappeared down the dark
street, I stopped at Stanley's Chrysler sedan to tell him.

Agent Fredericks sat in the front seat, working a computer
with one hand and talking on his radio, which he held with
the other.

"Hold it," he said into the radio when I rolled lopsidedly
up to his open door. Then to me: "What do *you* want?"

Whatever signs of friendship I had been enjoying with
Stanley were gone. I was responsible, it could be argued, for
his partner's death. That made for a big wall. And I was sorry.

"Pizza," I said quietly. "The blown-up car smells like pizza. Maybe it was the delivery car coming with our order."

"Maybe," he said coldly. "What's the name of the place?"

"Pizza Den. Colonial Drive."

"Ruth?" he said, his attention back to his radio. "After you send me a new team, call the Pizza Den on Colonial Drive here in Orlando and find out where their delivery person is and what kind of car they use. Call me back. Thanks."

"I'm sorry about Steve," I said when Stanley set the mike on his dashboard and returned to the small terminal on the seat beside him. It sounded totally unfitting and inadequate.

"It was his job." Agent Fredericks didn't even look up.

I pushed the gimpy wheelchair down toward the end of the block, retrieved the necessary supplies from my trunk, and rolled around between my front bumper and the back hatch of Brenda's Blazer. When I got to the curb and prepared to transfer out onto the grass, I discovered that I wasn't alone.

"Hi, Stick Man! My friend Rodney and I were just having a private little chat. Why don't you join us?"

"Rodney" sat with his back to the Blazer's rear right wheel. His hands were secured behind him. He started to appeal to me, but Butch clicked several times with the massive silver locking pliers in her right hand. Rodney thought better of his idea and remained quiet.

"Rodney," Butch said as I sat down in the grass next to her and popped off the quick-release axle on my right wheel, "do you know who this is?"

Rodney looked at me again, then at the chair, then nodded slowly.

"Rodney here blew up your house, Stick. Didn't you, Rodney?"

Rodney looked as if he was taking the fifth until the grating click of the locking pliers loosened his grasp on whatever constitutional rights he might otherwise have had. He nodded again.

"That's a good boy. And you just tried to blow up another house, didn't you?"

Another nod. I tossed the punctured inner tube up on the hood of my Camaro, poked the offending glass splinter back out of my tire from the inside, and ran my fingers around feeling for others before inserting the new tube.

"Mm. Stanley will want to talk to you, Rodney." I said.

"Well," Butch said, "we've been working on that, Rodney and I. You know, to make sure he doesn't forget anything when he talks to Mr. Fredericks. I wanted to avoid what happened with our friend Arfaad."

"I can see where that might be helpful."

"Sure, I thought you would. And just in case Rodney decides—later—not to share what he's shared with me, I promised that I'd hunt him down like a dog . . . wherever he is."

Rodney looked at me, his eyes pleading for reassurance that this wasn't really so.

"She'll hunt you down like a dog, Rodney," I said flatly. "Wherever you are. It's an ugly thing." The metallic clicking of the locking pliers punctuated my statement and brought an emotion-filled tear to Rodney's eye. I was touched. I snapped the pump nozzle onto my newly repaired tire and started working the handle. "Who's paying you, Rodney?"

"I already told *her*."

Butch clamped the pliers onto the man's nose so fast, I missed it. I looked up when he yelped and saw the pliers dangling from his snout.

"A woman! A woman!" he cried. "Get it off!"

"Seems to get his attention," Butch said, reaching up deliberately to release the silver handles.

"I can see how it would," I said.

"And who is this woman?" I asked Rodney, trying not to smile.

"I don't know. She calls on the pay phone . . . leaves money different places . . . half before, half after."

"And she wants you to dress up like that?" I said, pointing to the Arabic scarf on the ground next to Butch.

"Yeah. She pays an extra ten G's for that."

Ten thousand dollars extra to wear a scarf? Grief and conscience, I thought, that's some *serious* cash flow. I climbed back into my wheelchair and gathered up my stuff. "Well, Rodney," I said. "I don't think you're going to get a bonus this time. And that woman will probably have you killed—maybe by one of your own friends—just for being stupid enough to get caught. I'd be real helpful to Agent Fredericks if I were you. He just might be the only person who can keep you alive."

After Stanley and Rodney Johnson had a little talk, the agent locked the bomber securely in the backseat of his government-issue sedan to wait for a transport car. But not before exacting a pound of flesh.

"Watch it," Stanley said, gently guiding the man's head into the car, exactly as law enforcement training dictated. It was only after the FBI agent slammed the door shut that Butch and I became aware that Rodney's left foot was still on the outside. The scream was muffled inside the big sedan, so none of the neighbors took any notice. "Sorry," Stanley said, tripping against the door twice before managing to open it. "Weren't you in all the way? How clumsy of me."

Then Stanley shook Brenda's hand. "Thanks, Butch," he said. "I owe you one."

"Let's just find the woman who's paying him," Butch answered.

"Deal."

Back inside the cottage, everyone was busy but subdued. The house itself had been violated again. As foolish as it sounds, I could sense its deepened sadness. Peter was examining the small fireplace, with Mrs. Woods hovering nearby.

"That used to be the only source of heat," Edna said as

she paused to pick several tiny shards of glass out of the red and black area rug. "This was my father's house."

A hymn of similar designation came to mind and I hummed it to myself as I rolled over to check on Trish and Jerry, trying to digest what was happening to my life . . . to all of our lives. We'd nearly left "My Father's World" and paid a visit to *His* house tonight. Why? Who was that crazy? Or that angry? Especially since it *wasn't* Arfaad. Maybe it was personal for someone else too.

$\triangledown$

31

THE PRESS ARRIVED BEFORE Stanley's new agents, but he kept them outside, made a brief statement that none of us could hear well enough to understand, and promptly sent them packing. Soon two additional unmarked cars arrived. The first whisked Rodney away. An agent from the second vehicle went right to work on the dead car while her partner disappeared into the darkness that wouldn't last much longer.

"Yes!"

It was Trish Taylor, and her voice told the story. Stanley swept into the room behind me and we looked at the mess on the terminal screen.

"Look," Trish said. "Right here. I'd never have noticed it. There's only one code discrepancy, just enough, I'm sure, to crash the program."

"And still keep the byte count identical," Jerry added.

The gibberish on the screen meant nothing to me, and I said so. I knew I was looking at two windows, both showing part of the same value table, but they looked the same to me.

"Look closer, Stick," Jerry said with a laugh. "Right here. See it?"

I finally nodded and Stanley rolled his eyes. Everyone else gathered around to watch. The value table in the left window had the letter C nestled in the midst of a hundred other seemingly meaningless characters. In the same spot on the adjacent table, there was another C, but that one had a vertical line running right through the middle. It was like a big cent sign.

"Every destruct signal is right where it's supposed to be, all the code instructions are correct, and the tone signals, as Jerry calls them, haven't been changed at all. But that little cent sign switch," she said, smiling at Jerry, "might do just what you said, Stick . . . make the program crash on the spot."

"What about the backup programs?" Stanley asked.

"Well," Trish said, "anybody who could pull this off could probably replace all the backups too. Those chips just plug in. Who'd ever know?"

"If that's the case," I said, sorting through it out loud, "then until the time the virus—if it is a virus—kicks in, we have the only copy of the wrong program. And, after it kicks in, we'll have the only accessible copy of the right one. No wonder somebody's killing people for this disc."

"That's my bet," Jerry said. "Look, we'll just change the name of the right one, so we can keep them straight until we get it back to NASA."

"Well," Trish replied, "there's a bit of a rub on that count, Jerry. We discovered the *difference* between these two programs, but until they're tested, or compared to the ones in the system at the cape, there's no way of knowing which one is the 'right' one. Jim Woods could easily have designed it with either the C or the cent sign in that value table . . . we have no way of knowing."

Great.

At least the next shuttle launch was three months away.

Someone—a *woman*, I reminded myself—was working overtime, right *now*. The feeling of "time to spare" had disappeared when the car bomb went off halfway between the
Winter Park cottage and the street, but my growing sense of
urgency seemed, at once, both appropriate and unfounded.

"Stick," Todd called. "I'm in at the NASA board. Come
see if this message is what you wanted."

I read the note and the questions carefully. They were
close enough to what I wanted, and I slapped Todd on the
shoulder and told him so. Out the window, in the dim glow
of the yard light, I saw Gene Woods and Peter Stilles dragging
a sheet of plywood out of the blue and white aluminum storage shed that sat next to Edna's garden. Stanley came and
watched Todd over my shoulder.

"Anything on our lady friends?" I asked, hoping he wasn't
still hating me.

"Martha Denton squeaks worse than Woods did," he answered sourly. "That makes the back of my neck itch. The
only possible wrinkle is a slight increase in the number of
times she came back in after supper to work late, with a guest.
It's in the security guard's log book, just prior to the time
when Jim Woods was killed. But they tell me that happens a
lot. Anybody with Martha's clearance can bring family members or friends, as long as it's not during an actual launch.

"Willa Perkins has only one note on her local sheet. A
little old lady, two floors up and four condos over, 'happened'
to notice her sunbathing in the nude and called the Titusville PD. The officer who responded just told Ms. Perkins to
move one of her potted plants, and the old lady to watch
something else. He made notes, but didn't bother to ask for
any ID or file a formal report."

"When was that?"

"A little over a month ago. I'm running her on national
now, but since nothing else shows up here—she doesn't even
have a driver's license—there's not much chance that there's

a rap sheet on her anywhere else. The new systems are shared, and a record—even a little one—follows you everywhere."

"And Katie?"

"Stick, we ran Katie every which way to Friday. She doesn't exist before a fragmented junior college transcript in New York. But nobody there remembers her, even though she's in their computer file. Same thing at the liberal arts college in Beaver Falls, PA. I've had two agents working on Katie Newman day and night. Nothing but dead ends."

"What about Ren and Phyllis Catloth?"

"We talked to them twice. All they know is what Katie told them about her folks dying when she was twelve, and all that, but nothing, no details to hang anything concrete on. She was really attending classes there at KU, it seems, but as far as everything else goes, it's a professional cover job or I've never seen one. I'm sorry, Stick."

Stan the Man was back, a little, but I'd rather have had Agent god and still have been able to believe in Katie Newman. But then being foolish seems to get easier with practice.

"Stick?" Todd said. "Sorry to interrupt, but I've got two choices here." He pointed to the menu on the screen. "I can punch selection L and 'leave message for the sysop,' or I can choose W and, supposedly, wake the sysop. What'll it be?"

Stanley seemed unconcerned, but I knew without question. "Wake him up."

Butch Grady came in the front door, ushering in a resolute pizza delivery boy, a teenager whose acne-ravaged face and bare arms bore evidence of a losing struggle with the pavement.

"This is my new friend Joe. He and Rodney had a bit of a tussle earlier!"

"The pizza's free," Joe said, offering the boxes to anyone who'd take them. Jerry did. "I'm supposed to ask for Mr. Fredericks."

Stanley actually smiled and offered the boy his hand. "That would be me, Joe. I've just got to ask you some questions."

"I've got some questions too," Joe said bravely. "Like who *was* that bogus dude? And who's gonna pay for my car?"

Everyone smiled sadly.

"Oh, yeah, and Mr. Foster? Like I was wondering, if maybe I could be in your next column?"

"Page two, Joe!" I said with a laugh. "But you have to call me Stick."

"That's awesome, Stick! It's a deal!"

On that note, Stanley led the boy out to the kitchen, and my attention returned to Todd's project just as the terminal sounded three dings and flashed out a return message.

WAKING SYSOP NOW!

For a moment, the square black cursor just blinked on and off, the only sign of life on an otherwise tranquil screen. I shrugged and started to thank Todd for trying, but the flashing cursor began to march across the terminal's luminescent face.

Chat Mode. Sysop is now on-line, the parade of characters proclaimed.

After what seemed like several long minutes, new letters appeared, one after another, across the screen.

Before I can answer your questions, I'll need to know a little more about you, Todd, the voiceless system operator said, **and something about why you want this kind of information.**

Todd went right to work.

I'm a junior reporter for the *Melbourne Sun Coaster*, he typed. **I'm working with Stick Foster, and we may have figured out how someone could sabotage the fail-safe destruct software at the cape. Now we need to make an educated guess about which launch vehicles are the most likely to fall prey to the sabotage.**

Todd copied the sysop's lead and "returned" down two lines. This was, obviously, the BBS equivalent of "over."

We've heard a lot about Mr. Foster around these parts lately, the jogging letters admitted, **but I need something more concrete . . . something I can check out.**

Todd looked at me and shrugged. "He's a cautious one, Stick. Any suggestions?"

"Mm. Stanley!" I called out to the kitchen, "Can you help us here a minute?"

Before the FBI agent reached us, the bright characters moved once again.

You still there?

Yes, Todd's letters replied. **Hang on a minute.**

Stanley read the computer conversation and then took over the keyboard.

This is Agent Stanley Fredericks. FBI. Please call the following number, give my ID to the operator, and verify my location at this terminal's exchange. If necessary, cape security can also identify me in the same way. Your cooperation with Mr. Foster and Mr. Gulick would be appreciated.

Stanley rose and said that he would call in from the car so that his dispatcher would expect the inquiry.

Give me a minute or two, said the disembodied and silent voice on the computer before us. **End Chat Mode. Sysop is now off-line.**

There was nothing to do but wait.

When Stanley returned, moments later, he looked even harder around the edges than before. Something else had gone wrong, but I hesitated to ask what. I needn't have worried.

"We missed catching Rodney Johnson's next call," he said, fairly spitting with self-reproach.

"What call?"

"He was supposed to go back to his pay phone, wait for his secret employer's call, and report the success or failure

of his mission. I didn't even think of it! By the time the folks
in the Orlando office got around to that angle, it was too
late."

Storm clouds gathered around Agent god's head, and I
fought the desire to back away. "Would that have helped us
catch her?"

"Probably not," Stanley said, "but it might have kept our
friend from finding out that her hired thug had failed. Whoever she is, she's not one to back off and leave a job unfinished."

Mm.

Todd's terminal came back to life just then.

Chat Mode. Sysop is now on-line.

"Here we go," Todd announced.

Todd . . . you still there?

Go. Todd typed before punching the return key twice.

**On the backup question: navy jets with missiles *might*
be able to help early on, but after one of those rockets gets
up to escape velocity, I'm not sure any jet-launched missiles we've got could catch up. Beyond that, I don't know.**

**On the other . . . I'll post a bulletin and see what every-
body else thinks (I can't survey the BBS members at this
hour. And anyway, they have to call here.), but if I had to
guess, the crate going up in a couple of hours would get
the most votes by a landslide. It's a Central Dynamics *Excaliber*. In fact, it's the last *Excaliber*. Even IF it gets this
secret military payload successfully into space, nobody at
NASA will mourn its passing. Nothing but trouble since
the beginning . . . 6 out of 9 have had some kind of problem. 4 had to be blown.**

As Todd thanked the Panthers sysop and logged off, Stanley and I just stared at each other in horror. Who ever said
the saboteur *had* to go after a shuttle?

$\bigtriangledown$

32

WHEN IT SUNK IN, everyone panicked at once. Stanley started giving orders, demanding that he be given the disc and that Trish and Jerry accompany him to the cape at once. It wasn't a good time to interrupt god, but then when was it ever? I knew how my Dad would have answered, but he would have been talking about something all-together different.

"Stanley," I said, blocking the front door with my wheel-chair. "Wait a minute. Didn't you just say that our lady friend knows her latest terrorist attack failed?"

He nodded.

"Then her boys will likely be out there waiting for something like this, don't you think?"

Stanley nodded again, then sat in the chair by the door and cursed mildly.

"Okay, what about this then," I offered. "Trish, can you make backup copies of both programs on Jim's 3.5-inch floppy disks?"

She slid open the wooden rolltop disk file on Jim's desk and counted the contents. Jerry started rooting through the late wizard's desk. Between them they added used and un-

187

formatted storage disks, came up with a total, and divided
that by the number of 3.5-inch floppies it would take to hold
the present contents of their laser equivalent.

"Three," Trish said at last. "If we use everything he's
got—erase the old ones and format the new ones—we can
make three extra copies. With one floppy to spare."

I told them to save Jim's improved ComDat program. I
looked back at Stanley. "Four chances to make it through
sure beats one. What do you say?"

He let out a long breath and looked at everyone in the
quiet room. Their determined faces told him that they would
all help, willingly.

"Do it."

Stanley left with the first copy, but only after a heated telephone discussion with the military authorities now in
charge at the cape. No, they would *not* delay launching the
Excaliber. They obviously didn't care who Stanley was.
"Their people," the FBI man told us afterward, had tested
the system repeatedly and said there was "no evidence of a
problem." So, of course, there couldn't be a problem.

Stanley was steamed, but he called the Orlando police department and told them what was about to happen. They
promised to send help and pass the word to other law enforcement agencies along the route back to the cape. At last,
Stanley pointed at Jerry Wagner and stomped out the door
with a handful of floppy disks, promising that military heads
would roll. I hoped to myself that his and Jerry's remained
firmly attached. Out loud, I wished them luck. Stanley
paused, halfway down the front steps, and turned back to
face me.

"You'd better be careful, Foster. You and I aren't done yet."

What do you know, I thought. Stanley still cares.

"Call me Stick!" I called after him.

*   *   *

Todd and Butch Grady went next. Butch drove. Todd could, she assured him, pick up his car later. Todd looked very brave. And, I suspected, it wasn't all for Butch's benefit. The boy knew that what he was doing was important, maybe the most important thing he would ever do. Todd might be something of a geek, but he wasn't a coward.

Peter Stilles and one of the other FBI agents—a young woman named Jody Drake—carried me down the front steps before getting into the new government-issue Chrysler that sat parked, blocking the entrance to the driveway. Peter stuck his arm out the window and shook my hand. His palms were sweaty, but there was a burning intensity in his eyes.

"I want to beat these guys, Stick," he said. "For Phil."

"I know," I said. "Me too. Good luck."

Dennis Kane, the remaining FBI agent, Trish Taylor, and I hurried down the street to my Camaro. Dennis, a short, quiet, brown-haired man of about thirty, was carrying the laser read-write unit. He stopped about fifty feet from my car and held up his hand.

"Wait here."

Trish and I stood back while the young agent took a flashlight and searched my old car from top to bottom, inside and out.

"I've been watching it," he said, motioning us to join him, "up until Agent Fredericks called me inside. Just wanted to be sure."

Agent Kane suggested that Trish hunker down in the back, and he looked as if he were going to take the wheel, but I wouldn't have any of it.

"I appreciate the offer, Dennis, but if this turns out to be my last trip in this crate, I'm definitely going to be the one driving! How much time do we have?"

"Launch is in fifty-six minutes," Trish said as she helped pull my wheelchair into the back. "We're going to have to step on it."

"Okay," I said. "Let's do it."

I reached for the ignition, and at the same instant a distant explosion echoed through the morning darkness. It was followed by what sounded like cheap firecrackers and two more explosions. Then the eastside suburb was quiet once again. The hair rose on the back of my neck, and my underarms got moist in a hurry.

"Well," Dennis said bitterly, drawing a 10mm automatic pistol from inside his suit, "they're not out of bullets and dynamite quite yet, are they? Let's stay off the highway for a while. Do you know Goldenrod Road?"

I said I did, started the car, pulled a U-turn, and headed down the street in the opposite direction for several blocks before working my way back around to the east.

"Stanley?" Agent Kane said into his portable radio. "Do you read? Over."

Nothing.

Then the radio receiver crackled to life.

"Dennis? This is Jody. I can't raise him either, but I can see a fire off to the south. Out."

"Be careful," Dennis answered back unnecessarily. "Out."

While Dennis muttered curses under his breath and scoured the road ahead with a determined scowl, I began to pray. Despite what happened the last time, I found that the petition formed unbidden in my mind. Safety for the others, justice for the guilty, speed for my rusty Camaro. And life for my friends Stanley Fredericks and Jerry Wagner.

I worked my way through Maitland and Goldenrod before turning south toward Highway 50. When I reached the four lane and headed east, we could all see the fire far behind us. Sirens echoed dimly in the distance. Someone—probably Stanley—had sprung one trap. I wanted to believe it was the only trap, but only a fool would relax now. We were soon doing ninety miles per hour, and the Camaro hummed contentedly. The eastern sky was now ever-so-much lighter than the night behind us.

"Did I hear Agent Fredericks say that one of the suspects was called in for nude sunbathing?" Trish asked from the back.

"Yes," I said. "She's using the name Willa Perkins."

"Doesn't seem to me that nude sunbathing and terrorism fit into much of a type profile," Trish said with a laugh. "But today, who knows?"

"I can see the headlines," I said. "Hundreds Killed by Woman with Total Tan."

Then something clicked. Something Officer Mary Ellen Decker had told me during one of our late-night chats at the hospital. Some departments, like Titusville, left it to the investigating officer's discretion as to how much hard data they should collect and whether the incident warranted a full report. Other departments, she had said, required officers to do the whole nine yards on every call: loose dog, music too loud, children cutting across the lawn, everything.

"Hello?" the voice was right out of la-la land.

"Fonze," I said gently. "Wake up, buddy. I need some help."

"Foster? Is that you? Come here so I can shoot you down like an animal in the street."

"Good morning to you too. Listen, I'm here with Agent Kane. Agent Fredericks may be wounded. Can your computer run down calls by subject instead of by suspect?"

"Sure. Why?"

I told him my theory about the nude sunbathing thing and made him promise to check as many Florida police departments as possible. If Butch was right, and Willa had only been renting that condo for eight months, there was at least a chance. I thought back to Jim Woods's funeral and the striking woman at the back of the crowd. It was apparent from the deep brown color of her skin that Willa Perkins lay out on a regular basis and had probably done so for many years. Maybe, just maybe, she did it in the buff somewhere else—someplace where a more detailed report might have been taken when a concerned citizen looked just a little bit too hard.

"Call me back if anything turns up."

"Okay," Fonze said, sleepily. "I'll get right on it, but you owe me, Foster."

"Aw, Fonze, come on . . . call me Stick!"

When I hung up, Agent Dennis Kane cursed.

"Sorry, Dennis. Was it something I said?"

"Look in your rearview mirror."

I looked back. For a second, nothing registered. Then, at the edge of vision, a new column of flame reached toward the sky.

"You don't suppose its one of theirs, huh?" I asked without much hope.

"Not likely."

Great.

$\triangledown$

3 3

"DENNIS! COME IN! CAN you read me? Over."

Agent Kane sighed loud and long as he picked his radio up off the floor. "Got you, Jody. What's up?"

"We're down. I repeat, we're down. I took out the bad guys, but they trashed the car. Over."

"I read you, Jody. How's the civilian? Over."

"He's got a bump on the head, but he's okay."

"Stick?" Peter's voice crackled through the portable radio.

Dennis handed me the portable transceiver. "Just press the button on the side."

"Hi, Peter. Getting a little too exciting?"

"You're darned straight it is. You're gonna have to get 'em for me, Stick."

"I'll do my best, Peter." Agent Kane took back the radio.

"There'll be cops all over in a couple of minutes, Jody. Commandeer a ride and catch up when you can. Over."

"Got it. Out."

The digital clock on my stereo cassette deck told me that I had thirty-two minutes in which to drive forty-five miles. Considering the fact that I planned to fly straight through the approaching toll booths, I figured I could still make it. The Camaro purred like Butkis and ran toward the coastline like a Florida panther.

When the phone rang, Dennis got to it first.

"Speaking," he said. "Yes. Yes. Did you call an ambulance? The bureau office? Okay, thanks."

Not a promising dialogue. I asked Agent Kane about the bad news.

"The cops found Stanley and Mr. Wagner," he said slowly. "That was the first fire we saw. Several sticks of dynamite were dropped out of a car up in front of them. The first unit on the scene said that Stanley probably rolled his car trying to avoid it. An ambulance took them both to Florida Hospital in Winter Park. That's supposed to be a good one, isn't it?"

I knew every hallway by heart. The memories weren't very pleasant ones, but Dennis didn't need to know that. "The best," I said.

Two down, one up, one maybe. Dennis began getting radio messages, patched from the sheriff's department, the local police in each township we flew through, and from the Florida highway patrol. They were already blocking crossroads and clearing the road ahead. It was, they all promised, clear sailing all the way to the cape.

I pushed the Camaro up to 102 miles per hour, and the turbulent air whistled past the open window.

"You owe me a perm!" Trish said, leaning up to shout over the wind.

"We'll get Randy White to pay for it," I promised. "Just don't let that laser disc blow out of your hands."

"My fingerprints are permanently engraved on it, I think. I'm too old for this, Stick, and it's making me older by the minute. I've been thinking, though, if I survive this mad adventure of yours, I'm going to take that vacation I've been promising myself for years. How does Colorado sound?"

"Right now," I said, "Cleveland sounds good!"

"On the whole," Dennis put in, mimicking the late W. C. Fields quite well, "I'd rather be in Philadelphia."

We flew by the first patrol cars, which sat along the road with their lights turning in the cool morning air. Several flashed their headlights. As we passed under Interstate 95, out of the country and into a growing expanse of coastal developments, I had to slow down. We saw more and more law enforcement officers and they all waved or gave us a thumbs-up. Some hit the buttons on their radios and said, "Get 'em, Stick!" or "All clear, Stick!" A familiar voice crackled through the speaker, sounding like a grin. "Kick that computer where it hurts, Stick!"

We may have lost the mad bombers, but the launch was less than twelve minutes away as I approached the first toll booth. The normally wide opening seemed all wrong. At eighty miles per hour, it came at me like the eye of a small sewing needle. And I suddenly felt like a very fat piece of thread. When Dennis Kane covered his head with his arms and assumed the classic crash position against the dashboard, I lost my nerve and slowed down to sixty. Even so, the money takers bolted in panic, fleeing toward the flashing police cruisers on either side of the highway. The tiny buildings still shot passed in a blur, the air turbulence making a hollow popping sound in the open side windows.

The last toll booth put us on the hump-backed causeway bridge to the cape. I could see the *Excaliber*'s nose against the brightening eastern sky.

"There it is," I said. "We're almost there."

"Nine minutes," Trish Taylor said from the back. "Boy, will I be glad to get out of this car."

"Don't you like my driving, Trish?"

"Actually, Stick, even on a good day, my youngest son can't drive as well as you do. And he's probably about your age and he doesn't have a disability. No, I may be an old fuddy-duddy, but hunkering down back here while we're trying to outrun bombs and machine guns isn't my idea of fun."

I cranked down the long NASA employee entrance road and sped through the open gate, into the lot. I parked next to Dave Bentley's stepside pickup. As I climbed into my chair, while Trish stretched and attempted to bring some order to her hair and Dennis straightened his three-piece suit, it occurred to me that we might have trouble getting in despite the fact that Dennis and Stanley's superiors were to have cleared the way. I needn't have worried. We rushed through the double glass doors, past the empty guard station, and on toward the elevators.

Following a high-tech wheelchair down a long, smooth-floored corridor is no easy matter for an able-bodied individual. It's not quite a full-run speed, but it makes for an extremely invigorating fast-walking trot. Trish began to huff and puff before we were halfway down the hall. Just before we turned the corner, she gave it up, told us to hold the elevator, and fell back into a more comfortable pace.

"I can't install this if I die before I get there," she said in a winded voice.

Dennis broke into the awkward jog and held his shoulder holster still with one hand and carried the laser unit with the other. I beat him to the call buttons, pushed the top one, and spun back to see how Trish was coming. She had not yet rounded the corner at the end of the corridor, so I turned to congratulate Agent Kane on his racing form.

It didn't occur to me, until it was too late, that there hadn't been any security—regular or military—at the employee gate or inside the double doors. I thought of it only after I heard a sound behind me, like the soft splat of a rubber car mat being dropped on a concrete garage floor. Dennis's eyes got big as a small red dot appeared suddenly in the center of his forehead.

$\bigtriangledown$

34

Dennis just crumpled onto the floor in front of me. Dead. I wasn't excited about turning back around, but I didn't want to die without knowing who'd killed us. I probably wouldn't have made it, except for the fact that Trish Taylor came huffing around the far corner then. By the time I spun the lightweight wheelchair back around, Tan Woman's gun was rising steadily, away from me and toward the winded computer specialist with the golden laser disc in her hand.

"Look out, Trish! Run!"

I threw my weight forward, taking a long downward stroke on the handrims. The chair shot forward, but Willa Perkins was at the next corner, maybe ten feet away. I had to stroke again. The gun went off before I got there, but a hissed curse told me she had missed. Tan Woman took off, obviously not as concerned with the helpless cripple as with the laser disc she had killed so many people to retrieve. That was a mistake. I had speed. I had momentum. And I was really pissed. I lunged out of my chair as she went by, burying my right shoulder in her abdomen and clamping my arms around her hips . . . just like my high school football coach had taught me.

A rush of wind burst from her mouth, her pistol clattered onto the floor and I heard it slide away in Trish's direction as I landed hard on top of her. She smelled of cocoa butter. I fully expected Willa Perkins to lie still, such was the ferocity of my tackle. I was wrong. Dead wrong.

She used my own momentum, kept me moving with a sharp kick-up of her right leg, and tossed me over her head and out onto the floor behind her like a beach ball. By the time I gathered myself together and struggled into a sitting position against the wall across from the elevator, she had retrieved her weapon. I looked straight into the silenced muzzle, knew I was dead, and thought the absurd: Hell hath no fury like a woman tackled.

"You just don't give up do you?" she asked. "Normally I might find that trait admirable, but today I have to shoot you. You deserve worse, but I haven't the time to waste on you. You've gotten in my way for the last time."

I saw the catlike blur and knew that I had to keep the Tan Woman's attention just a second longer. "Does Martha even know?" I asked.

At the name of her supposed lover, her lips curled with contempt. She started to speak, but Butch Grady hit her hard from behind. The pistol discharged before it clattered across the floor for a second time, and I heard the bullet ricochet harmlessly off several walls. I scrambled toward my chair and turned it upright just as the two women broke free, rose to their feet, and began circling each other slowly. Both grinned viciously.

After jumping back on board, I rolled down the hall and picked up the gun. But by the time I turned back toward the combatants, any hope of shooting Willa Perkins without endangering my friend had disappeared. Brenda "Butch" Grady had met her match. The sharp exchanges were brutal, but it was clear that both women were merely probing, testing each other for weakness. Arfaad had been a walk in the park by comparison, and I hoped that Butch was up to it. If not, I thought, glancing at Dennis Kane's still body, I would shoot Tan Woman without any reservation at all. That's when I remembered Trish Taylor. That's when I remembered the rocket probably was lifting off its launch pad while I sat mesmerized, like a Roman spectator watching the gladiators fight for their lives.

"Todd took Trish up the stairs," Butch said. She caught a blow that might have broken her nose but kicked Tan Woman sharply in the ribs. "Go!" she said, barely blocking Willa's counterattack.

I gathered up the laser unit, piled it on my lap with the deadly pistol, and pushed the elevator button. At least I would take the gun with me, out of Willa's reach. Not being able to help Butch didn't do much for my ego, but I tried to rationalize the value of the experience by assuring myself that I was more enlightened for having to roll away and leave Butch to fend for herself. She was certainly more capable than I. As the elevator carried me to the next floor, I decided that I could at least send down security. And Todd, of course, was probably already hurrying back. But then, I thought, as the elevator doors opened, Todd would have little better chance against Tan Woman then I had. In a perverse way, I found that thought comforting.

The sight of the camo-bedecked soldier on guard outside the flight-tracking control room doors should have been comforting too. But it wasn't. In retrospect, there were all manner of things wrong: the length of his hair, the Mac-10 minigun instead of an M-16, and the worn and dirty boots. In that instant, however, only the flimsy, lifelike rubber mask registered in my conscious thought. Even as he spun the muzzle of the tiny machine gun toward my chair, I dove to the right, letting the laser box go and clutching for the handgun on my lap.

The barrage of bullets ripped through the black nylon upholstery and clattered off the floor and walls behind me. I pointed and shot wildly, nothing but adrenaline guiding my actions. So when the man collapsed, clutching his chest, I was astonished. And when two of his buddies came out of the control room door, I was, at least, waiting for them with the pistol steadied across the tattered seat of my newly ventilated wheelchair. The first masked figure tripped over his fallen comrade, so the woman behind caught the bullet I'd intended for him.

Something cold, calculating, and scary crept across my mind and heart as I watched him struggle to gain control of his weapon with both hands and train it on me. The rest had been instantaneous self-preservation, some kind of instinct to survive. This, however, was different. Time seemed to stand still.

The scene played itself out in slow motion. I sat there on the floor, filled with rage. My arms were stretched out across the seat cushion of my damaged chair, the top of the man's head squarely in my gun sights, and I just waited for him to make me shoot. It took forever. His masked face and his machine gun barrel came up off the floor together, and I was already squeezing the trigger when his eyes met mine. If I had been holding Joe Stetler's hair-trigger automatic, the man would have died then and there.

Instead, his eyes opened wide, and he took his left hand off the gun and raised both arms off the floor in an acknowledgment of defeat. I eased my trembling finger back off the trigger and started to relax. That's when he shot me. He brought the minigun down with one hand and fired a burst that enveloped me in a hissing breeze. I pulled the trigger of Willa's pistol without even being aware that I had done so. Fortunately it was still pointed directly at the gunman's head, and the machine gun fire stopped abruptly.

At least two of the terrorists were still alive. As the echoes of gunplay died away, I heard their moans, cringed at the sound of their ragged breathing. I was wounded too, but I didn't dare look away. There were too many weapons in the small pile of bodies down the hall, and two too many bad guys still alive beside them. I could do nothing about the sharp, burning pain in my left armpit. I couldn't even climb back in my chair. Who would come out the door next, I thought. How many more were there? How many bullets were left in Tan Woman's gun? How many more people did I have to shoot? Newspaper reporters aren't supposed to shoot people, but I kept the gun pointed at the door anyway.

This time it opened slowly. I watched it swing out until it stopped against the last terrorist's foot. I tried to keep the pistol steady, anticipating where the next attacker would appear through the opening, but the shakes were getting worse and my own sweat burned in my eyes. When a cautious face peered around the doorjamb and looked anxiously in my direction, I cried for joy. Tears came from out of nowhere and ran down my face as the tension rolled away.

"Am I glad to see you, Todd," I said. "Get their guns."

Todd kicked several weapons away as he stepped out over the fallen intruders, followed by Dave Bentley and several disheveled but definitely genuine military officers who promptly gathered up the arsenal. He looked at the carnage, then back at me.

"You did this?"

"I think I'll take the fifth on that, Todd."

"You're hit!"

I set the pistol on the floor beside me and looked down at my left side. The blood had soaked through my shirt, but as soon as I leaned away from the chair to get a better view, the worst of the pain ceased abruptly. "I'm okay. It's just a scratch," I said. "You'd better go down and check on Butch."

That really got Todd moving. He looked me over quickly before the bullet-riddled elevator door opened, then called to the dazed PR man who stood gaping at the battlefield. "Help him out down here, Dave," Todd said. "I'll be right back."

Dave Bentley, clearly rattled, walked slowly down the hall toward me while I wrapped the two broken wheel spokes around their nearest neighbors several times. That would get them out of the way until I could take the tire off and replace them. Being stabbed by a sheared-off bicycle spoke isn't as heroic sounding as taking a bullet, but I thanked God for my good fortune. The story value didn't matter at all.

"Are you really okay?" Dave asked, offering me a hand back into my tattered wheelchair. "Look at this thing. You mean all that shooting and they just shot up your chair?"

"It looks that way," I said, checking myself over again. "What's going on inside?"

"Well, I don't know. The bird just went up when the shooting started."

"Okay, how about picking up that laser gizmo? I hope it still works."

When the real soldier types cleared the doorway, I rolled in and set Dave Bentley and a nearby technician to the task of installing the laser device. That started Trish Taylor and Martha Denton into a heated battle of their own. Trish waved the golden disc, insisting that Martha load the data immediately. While the giant *Excaliber* rocket climbed across a dozen television monitors, Ms. Denton's underlings, along with several military specialists, seemed to be taking Trish's side in the dispute. Martha Denton, however, ruled this particular roost. She reminded everyone that she had personally checked the communication software herself. Several times.

"Ms. Denton?" I said, rolling up beside her.

"You!"

"Yes, it's me. Did you ever bring Willa Perkins here?"

At the name of her lover, Martha's face blanched and her breath caught in her throat.

"She's paying these terrorists and she replaced the old

ROM fail-safe chips with new ones. She had Jim Woods killed, Martha, because he had the only comparable copy of both the original and the virus-infected replacement."

"No!"

There was a loud shuffling behind us, and I turned in time to see the real soldiers, along with Todd Gulick, back into the room with their hands up. Willa Perkins, barely recognizable behind the cuts and contusions on her tan face, marched in after them. She held Dennis Kane's 10mm automatic fast against Butch Grady's neck and used the battered bartender's body as a shield.

"You!" she yelled at Trish Taylor. "Bring me that disc. Now!"

There were sirens in the distance. Someone had used the respite to call for help. Willa was in a hurry, and no one in the room failed to recognize the dangerous look in her eyes. She took the disc, stuck it in her pocket, and started backing out the door, pulling Butch with her.

"If anyone follows me, she dies."

Before she disappeared from sight, Willa Perkins looked directly at Martha Denton and sneered in disgust. Then she was gone.

▽

35

Martha Denton stood there like a marble pillar. The room turned to stone all around her, although the men by the door seemed to be tensed, counting, waiting for some signal that it was safe to take up the chase. Todd suddenly broke the spell, swept up one of the miniguns by the wall, and burst out the door. I cringed. Todd Gulick had never fired a gun in his life. Martha swayed slightly, her eyes glazed over. She seemed to be holding her breath. I reached out to steady her.

"Martha? Are you all right?" It was a stupid question.

"System failure!" A young man's voice rang out in the silence. "The bird's starting to wobble!"

"RSO's report fail-safe failure!" stammered the disbelieving voice of a woman to our right.

"Martha!" Trish said, taking the stupefied computer specialist by the shoulders. "We've got to do something. Now!"

"It's too late." The words were a whisper, barely audible in the chaos.

Trish pushed past the bewildered woman and sat down at Martha's console.

"Range safety officers still calling in!" shouted the same woman to my right. "What do I tell them, Ms. Denton?"

"Martha," I said as calmly as I could, "it's not too late. This is Trish Taylor. She works at Morton, and she has a copy of the right program, but you've got to help her." Trish was already feeding the first of the 3.5-inch floppy disks into the NASA computer.

"The bird's staring to turn!" shouted the first young man. "Do something!"

"RSO's are pushing all the right buttons," the women to my right shouted back, "but nothing's happening. Somebody give me a backup!"

Martha Denton's eyes never moved. She just stared at the doorway where her life had come unglued. "It's my fault . . . all of it."

"No, Martha," I said, taking her hand. "You were used. Used by a pro. But you can still beat her."

"Backup on-line!" yelled a third voice.

"Nothing!" came the answer. "Give me another!"

"Martha, listen to me." I squeezed her hand hard, and tugged gently on her arm. "None of the backups will work. We think Willa switched all the chips with ones that were programmed to crash this morning, but we can fix it. You can fix it. But it's got to be now!"

Trish was halfway through the pile of gray plastic disks, feeding them in one at a time, dumping the data and removing them as fast as she could.

"They're sending fighter jets!" someone called out.

"Why not just throw rocks at it?" another voice added sarcastically.

"Well, maybe at the apex . . ." the first voice said hopefully.

"You gotta be kidding!" came the retort. "This baby won't slow down, stop, and begin falling back. She's gonna make the turn at top speed . . . and then start going even faster!"

Martha's gaze dropped slowly. I kept pulling on her arm until she looked at me. "I was such a fool." Tears ran down her face, but she remained motionless.

"Yes, Martha. You were a fool. We've all been fools. But don't be a fool again."

A chorus of disappointment echoed around the room, and I looked up at the closest monitor. None of the missiles even came close. I could see them flitting uncertainly around the wobbling juggernaut, always falling behind. The rocket was over the top now, starting back toward earth.

"They're both loaded on the hard drive," Trish shouted at me over the panicked din, "but I don't know how to put them on-line!" She looked searchingly at the technicians around her, but they were all staring at the monitors or at Martha Denton, perhaps waiting for the resident wizardess to act.

"It's coming home," commented one technician, "and it's coming home fast."

"Where's it going?" someone yelled.

"Here, maybe. Maybe west of here," answered a man at the radar screen behind me. "Probably west. Three minutes, max."

I looked back at Martha's face, willing her to focus on my eyes. "Please, Martha, no matter what you've done, it's nothing compared to letting innocent people die. This rocket's headed for Disney World, Martha." I didn't know if it really was and the idea sounded ludicrous, but it was all I could think of. And it worked.

"Disney World?" Her eyes wandered toward the nearest monitor.

"Yes! Think about it, Martha. Do you want to let Willa Perkins get away with that?"

Her eyes glazed over again. I was losing her. "Martha, listen to me. Do you want to let her beat you?"

"No," she whispered. "No, I don't."

"Good! That's good! Now help Trish install these two programs. Please hurry."

"A minute and a half," said the man behind me. "And it just might land on Cinderella's Castle too."

Trish offered Martha back her chair. "Here and here," she said, pointing to files she had named c and ¢.

"They look the same," Martha whispered, noting the storage figures.

"They're not. Believe me," I pleaded. "Please put them both on-line, Martha."

As if some religious cult service were beginning, the people around us who stood staring at the thundering picture of death began, in ones and twos, to clasp their hands to their chests. Everyone knew they probably were safe, but Orlando was about to experience a catastrophe that could make recent worldwide earthquakes pale by comparison. And that, irrespective of what the SECRET military payload was.

"I can only load one at a time." Martha's voice came from a deep dark void. We were losing her.

"There's only time for one try anyway," said the guy behind us. "Do something *now*!"

I looked at Trish, asking her with my eyes. She just shrugged helplessly.

"Forty-five seconds to impact!"

"Dear God, help us!" I said out loud. I'd probably asked for too much too often lately, but whether it was coincidence or divine providence, I suddenly knew the answer.

"Cent sign!" I shouted. "Martha, run the cent sign! Hurry!"

Trish and I willed Martha to hurry. She was half in a stupor, but years of experience guided her numb fingers. The ponderous seconds dragged on while the thundering bird kept coming. Ironically, it had stabilized now that it was going in the wrong direction. When Martha's computer screen finally flashed that the upload was complete, the lady on the radio shouted, "Now! Go!"

For almost a second, nothing happened. The hurtling rocket was a wildly bouncing blur on the screen, chase planes and ground cameras going to the limit trying to keep it in the frame. Then, in a glorious string of explosions, the great bird disintegrated before our eyes. The room exploded too. There were shouts and cheers, and Martha's co-workers gathered around her, patting her on the back and praising whatever it was she had done. She looked at me, pleadingly.

"Take me outside, please."

"Sure, Martha," I said, motioning people out of our way. The hallway was filled with cops, deputies, and highway patrolmen. There were uniforms from at least four different precincts. They'd been watching and listening. Cheers and applause met us as we moved toward the elevator. Martha's eyes rose slowly.

"They really hate me," she whispered. "All of them."

"No, Martha," I said as the elevator doors opened. "You just saved Disney World."

She laughed sadly, and I sensed that she wouldn't make it much farther. When the doors opened, Officer Mary Ellen Decker stepped up and took Martha under the arm.

"Good job, Stick Man!"

"She needs help, Mary Ellen," I said. "Be gentle."

"There's an ambulance outside."

The paramedics helped Martha Denton into the red and white meat wagon, and Mary Ellen got in beside her. One of the crew gently slipped a blood pressure cuff around Martha's frail arm. The computer specialist looked at me, searching for peace I thought, as the first door closed. I held up my hand, stopped the other door, and stuck my head inside.

"You did good, Martha," I said. "Thanks."

It wasn't a smile. The poor woman probably didn't know how. But maybe, with professional help, someday.

Officer Decker gave me thumbs-up and a wink before the door shut and the ambulance pulled away.

While official people came and went in a great hurry around me, the aftershock hit me like a falling rocket. It got harder to breathe and I felt light-headed, about to fall out of my chair. I hurried over to the old Camaro and plopped into the relative safety of the bucket seat. I *had* to go see about Butch and Todd. Instead, I passed out.

$\triangledown$

36

I WOKE UP ON a gurney in the Titusville General emergency room. The Fonze jumped to his feet and brought me a glass of orange juice and a doughnut.

"How's this for a story, Stick? Melbourne cop fired for serving doughnuts in Titusville while on duty!"

I must have hesitated too long.

"They told me to make you eat and drink . . . or shoot you. Which will it be?"

I took the doughnut and the juice. "What happened?"

"Exhaustion. That's all. When did you sleep or eat last?"

"I'm not sure."

"Well, there you go. Eat!"

I ate.

"What about the others, Butch Grady and Todd?" I asked between bites. "Are they okay?"

"They're upstairs. They're gonna be fine," Fonze said. "I'm supposed to take you up there later. Here."

I took the newspaper from him and was shocked by three things: a fuzzy but full-color picture of the *Excaliber* coming apart, both a column and an article written by "me" (clearly Randy's work), and the fact that it was a Special Evening Edition. I searched the emergency room walls until I found a clock.

"Six-thirty! How'd it get to be six-thirty?"

The Fonze laughed. "You've been sleeping like a baby, Stick!"

The debris from the trashed *Excalibur* came down all over central Florida. It broke windows, dented cars, and cut up the flora and fauna, here and there, like a Vegomatic from outer space. Miraculously, however, no injuries to humans had been reported thus far. TV and radio bulletins, along with local police and their vehicle-mounted electronic bull-horns, were credited with keeping the relatively few early risers indoors. Disney World's 27,000 acres did, in fact, take the heaviest shower of space junk; but, of course, the famous theme park was not yet open for business at that time of the morning. I thanked God again that Martha Denton hadn't thought of that. Then, in a bizarre bit of reflection, it occurred to me that the world famous efficiency of Disney's maintenance personnel had surely been put to the test.

"You're a bone fide hero, Stick," Fonze said. "How does it feel?"

"I don't know." I suddenly remembered something important. "Did they get Willa Perkins, Fonze?"

"No. And nobody knows how, for sure, she got away. The leading theory is that she had some scuba gear hidden down along the canal behind the complex. The navy and the water patrol have been on it all day."

"What about the search I asked you to run?" I said, lifting my legs, one at a time, off the rolling table and transferring into my shot-up rolling chair.

"Nothing, I'm afraid." He took a folded piece of computer paper out of his uniform shirt pocket and gave it to me. "There were dozens of nude sunbathing complaints with complete police reports filed, but nothing unusual or notewor-thy about any of them. Only three even came close to the phys-ical description you gave me. They all checked out at their respective addresses. No terrorist-type nudists I'm afraid."

I scanned the two-page list without a clear idea of what I wanted to find. Of the three names circled, however, one leapt off the page and bit me on the nose. Bingo!

"This is it, Fonze! We've got her!"

"Are you off your nut, Stick? A Palm Beach princess?"

"Where's Jody Drake? You know, the FBI agent."

"I don't know. This is crazy. The Palm Beach PD called and checked her out."

"Yes, but did they go there or telephone? Did they talk to Wilma P. Worthington herself, or did they talk to her mother, or one of her maids?"

"I don't know, but come on, Stick. 'Gun toting, well-tanned, Palm Beach heiress terrorizes central Florida' is kind of a stretch, isn't it?"

"Maybe not. If I'm right, she's got the money, the industrial connections, the motive, and the past mental trauma to be our terrorist queen. I've gotta call Jody." I rolled through the drawn curtains and down the hallway to the nurses' station and asked for the phone. Everyone was looking at me and smiling. A few people said "Nice going, Stick." I didn't have time to be embarrassed. Several reporters, one with a camera crew, sprang into action as soon as I left the sanctuary of my room in the ER.

"Can you put them off a little longer, Fonze?"

"I can try," he said, turning to head them off. "Once more into the breach!"

The FBI dispatcher put me through to Agent Drake. She was back at the Federal Building in Orlando.

"How are you doing?" she asked.

"Better, thanks. What about Stanley and Jerry?"

"They were beat up pretty good in the wreck," she said, "but they'll be okay."

"Look, Jody," I whispered, "does the name 'Worthington' mean anything to you?"

"I don't think so, why?"

"What about Major Tom Worthington?"

"Oh, yeah, wasn't he the astronaut married to the social-ite down in Palm Beach? He died in some kind of an accident, I think."

"That's right. It was a secret test flight of some kind, and I remember reading something about his having a daughter in the air force, training to be an astronaut."

"Okay, so?"

"So I asked a local cop to run down all the nude sunbath-ing complaints and look for similar physical descriptions. One of them is a Wilma P. Worthington of Palm Beach. She'd have everything at her fingertips."

"Are you sure you want to work for a newspaper, Stick?" Jody laughed. "That's another handsome piece of field-work!"

"Well you guys better get on it. Lots of us saw her face, so she's probably moving out fast."

"We're on our way. Thanks!"

I spoke briefly to my media colleagues, careful to mention nothing about my latest suspicions. I didn't need a lawsuit. Then Fonze took me upstairs, where I rolled into Todd's room and was greeted by most of what the press was calling the Stick Foster Gang.

Todd had a patch on the side of his head, and his left shoulder was heavily bandaged, the arm in a sling. Butch sat nearby in a clunky hospital wheelchair, her face a mess and a broad piece of white tape plastered across her nose, but those startling blues were alight with new fire. She and Todd were holding hands. Trish sat in the room's only "comfy" chair like a matriarch holding court, and Peter sat on the floor by her feet, a light purple bruise ringing his right eye and extending halfway up his forehead. I passed quips of greeting to each until I recognized the lone figure sitting behind them on the windowsill. Anger and confusion welled up inside me, and I was about to say something nasty. Butch stopped me.

"She saved our butts, Stick. And she works directly for the Secretary of Defense. No lie."

I looked in Katie Newman's eyes, but I knew they'd never be the same. Even the Jayhawk was gone.

"I'm sorry, Stick," she said, "I couldn't say anything."

I turned back toward the bed, swallowed hard, and changed the subject, asking about Tan Woman's escape.

"She's been well-trained in martial arts," Butch said begrudgingly. "I'll give her that."

"Air force," I said. I could feel Katie stir at my remark.

"Really?" Butch went on. "Well, I'd rather take on six drunk guys any day."

"So, what happened to you, Todd Man?" I asked.

"She shot me," Todd said indignantly. "Twice!"

Everybody chuckled, and Butch told the story again for my benefit. Todd and the military contingent had split up by floors; Todd got the basement. It seems he rushed in on Tan Woman as she was about to finish Butch off and make good her escape. He yelled what Butch admiringly called a battle cry, leveled the Mac-10 at the terrorist's heart, and pulled futilely on the safety-locked trigger. Tan Woman promptly shot him twice for his efforts before turning her attention back to Butch, who's struggling undoubtedly saved Todd's life.

"That's when Katie showed up," Butch finished. "They shot at each other some before Willa jumped into the duct system and disappeared."

There was a long silence as we looked at each other and considered what we'd been through.

"We were nuts," I said at last.

"Crazy," Peter added.

"Certifiable," Todd said flatly.

"Yes," Trish Taylor said, pushing herself up out of her

chair, "but we were *good*, weren't we?"

There was some laughter, some hugging and some tears before we broke it up. Fonze said my car was parked in the wheelchair spot outside ER, so I offered Peter and Trish each a ride. I was going to see Stanley and Jerry anyway.

"I'll take Peter to Melbourne," the Fonze said. "I gotta go back to work anyway. You can head straight over to Orlando from here. Do you still know the way?"

Everybody laughed.

"More to the point," Trish added, "do you remember how to go the speed limit?"

Katie Newman caught up with us in the hallway. "Trish?" she said. "Can I talk to Stick alone for a minute?" The nickname sounded like a foreign word.

"That's up to him, Ms. Newman. Meet you in the car," she said, patting me lightly on the shoulder before walking on.

"Look," Katie started, "I never meant to—"

"Were you really going to marry him?" I interrupted. "Or was that part of the job too?" It stung her, hard. I was immediately sorry, and said so.

"No," she said. "I had that coming. Getting close to him—to see if he was okay—was part of my job. Falling in love wasn't."

The silence had hard broken edges. I couldn't look at Katie's face. "Who are you really?"

"I can't tell you." I heard the strain in her voice and looked up from the colored lines on the hospital hallway floor. "Look, I never met anybody like Jimmy in my whole life. He was just plain good, Stick. Honest, kindhearted, and gentle . . . like you." Tears filled her eyes, and she looked away. "Who needs that crap anyway!"

She stalked off down the hallway and disappeared around the corner. Katie Newman—whoever she was—was far too good at disappearing.

$\triangledown$

37

TRISH AND I DIDN'T talk much on the drive back to Orlando. There wasn't much to say. Forty-six law enforcement officers left me a Far Side card with a picture of a young gang of mounted cowboys gathered around a comrade who had, along with his trusty steed, crashed head-on into a tree. The card was covered with fond wishes, congratulations, and signatures. The caption said: "What are you going to tell your dad?"

I'm sure the cops knew before I did that there would be a toll to be paid. It crept over me as the miles slipped by. I'd pushed Mullet and Jeff out of my mind, but shooting five people, killing two of them, doesn't just go away. My two years in the army had, at least, introduced me to the concept, forcing me to think about the possibility. But the reality was something else. I tried to think about Phillip Stilles, Steve Lopez, Dennis Kane, and the guards at Leavenworth and the cape. It helped some. But not much.

I was used to handling big life changes, I decided stoically. I would handle this one too. I'd get over it. Why did it matter that I'd shot a woman? Tan Woman was an equal opportunity employer. The last man's face, the look in his eyes, that one was going to stay with me for a long time. Just thinking about it made me shudder.

Meghan sat by Jerry's bedside, holding his hand. He looked awful, strung up six ways in his monkey-bars bed, but the nurses had assured Trish and me that the traction was only a precautionary measure. There was no spinal cord damage.

"I'm sorry," I said to both of them. "It all kind of got out of hand, didn't it?"

"You did just fine," Meghan said, surprising me. "All of you. I'm so proud."

That helped. After visiting a while, and after Meghan offered to take Trish home, I excused myself, slipped out, and rolled down the familiar hall to Stanley's room. Or I should say, my room.

"Good old 207!" I said to Agent god. "Are you keeping up the proud tradition?"

Stanley looked up and smiled. "Now that you're a big-time national hero," he said, grimacing as he struggled to sit up, "they're talking about retiring the number. But if you mean am I going to leave here in a wheelchair, the answer is: no thank you."

"Can't say as I blame you. Look, Stan, I'm really sorry . . . about everything. Steve, Dennis, you—"

"That's enough of that. We're just dumb civil servants, but we're proud of what we do. And you were right all along. It rankles to be outpaced by the press, but you're more than just a reporter, Stick. You've got the knack. I don't like to think about what would have happened if you'd let me storm out of Jim Woods's house with the only copy of that program. Anyway, here."

I took the curled sheet of white paper and noticed that Stan the Man was smiling big time. The fax was clearly a picture of Willa Perkins/Wilma P. Worthington. Scrawled across the likeness was a well-reproduced handwritten message: "Tell Stick Foster that we got her! —J.D."

"We also found Arfaad," Stanley said. "Tan Woman's mercenary army of phony Arabs rescued him, cut his throat, and dumped him in a ravine in the middle of the Flint Hills before ditching the helicopter in an oil field near Emporia, Kansas. He made a very convincing decoy for a while."

"Do you know the deal about her dad's death?" I asked.

"No, but it was definitely a hushed-up affair. Add to that her getting bounced out of the astronaut program and the air force shortly thereafter when her sexual preferences were discovered, and you've got one angry little rich girl."

"But all this?" I said. "She didn't just get mad, did she?"

"No," Stan said, "and her Palm Beach estate is full of Ben Holcum material. The press is going to have a field day with her diary; she sees herself as Senator Holcum's 'right hand of justice.' Holcum is already spitting all over himself, swearing he knew nothing about her!"

"I don't suppose you'd consider leaking a copy of that diary?"

"Well," Stanley said with a grin as he pulled several more fax sheets out of the drawer in his bedside table, "as long as you promise not to print any of it until I clear you. We don't want to screw up any evidence, do we?"

"No, sir! Oh, and do we know where she got the chips made?" I asked.

"Mommy owns a factory out in Silicone Valley."

"How convenient."

A nurse stepped into the room and told me that visiting hours were over. Stanley Fredericks offered his hand and I took it proudly.

"By the way, Stick," he said. "How'd you know which program was the right one?"

"I didn't. But I think I know Jim Woods," I told him with a shrug, "and Jim Woods's gift, no his passion, was streamlining programs in any way possible. He was famous for speeding things up. Well, in music, a C stands for four-four time. Put a slash through it and it becomes two-four or half time."

"That was *really* reaching, Stick."

"I know, but it just came to me and felt right somehow."

"If you ever want a job—"

"No way!"

On my way out of the hospital, I rolled past the dark and quiet physical therapy gym, pausing to look in at the recently purchased high-tech weight machines and the full-body tilt table that was used to help the longtime bedridden patients regain their equilibrium, a little bit at a time. In the corner, against the wall, sat an architect's wooden drafting table. It was raised about forty degrees and covered with coarse sandpaper. In the center of the incline sat a large, rectangular plywood box with round handles sticking out both sides. There was, I knew, sandpaper on the bottom of the box too.

On my first visit to the PT gym (after I had regained the ability to sit upright without passing out!), they made me push that empty box up and pull it back down the table ten times. I almost didn't make it. Within a week, they were adding small bags of lead shot to the box. By the time I left to go home, it took three therapists, one to hold all the bags of lead shot in the overflowing plywood box and two to hold the drafting table against the wall. They weren't happy hours, I decided, but they were hours well spent. They helped me sort out what was real from what was not. Life is like that sometimes; good things, real things, are worth some effort . . . and some risk.

I stopped at a pay phone in the lobby.

"Hello?" the warm voice answered.

"I want to ask you a favor," I said.

"Anything."

"Can I come over?"

"Anytime."

"I could use a hug about now."

"Okay," Sam said, "but I might never let you go."

"I'll take my chances."